# Tigress for Two

## Alaskan Tigers: Book Three

Marissa Dobson

Published by Sunshine Press

Printed in the United States of America

ISBN-13: 978-1-939978-15-8

# DEDICATION

To Thomas—my wonderful husband who's been supportive through everything. He's put up with my late night writing sessions, cooked dinner, over all he's been wonderful. Thank you Thomas.

To my readers who love the Alaskan Tigers as much as I enjoy writing them. Enjoy this newest adventure to Alaska.

Tigress for Two: Alaskan Tigers

# Contents

*A life lived in fear...*

Kallie lived her life hiding from everyone and everything except selected members of her clan, fearing someone would discover who she was and what she had fled. She would not be tortured again, no matter if the cost was her life. When Taber enters her life, she isn't sure if she should trust him or run as fast and as far as she can. His presence changes everything, and to let him in means she must remove the guards keeping her safe since her escape.

*A debt that is owed...*

Taber owes the Alaskan Tigers more than he could ever repay. They supported him and his Kodiak bear sleuth when they needed backing the most. He has joined their fight against the rogue tigers in order to repay his debt. Finding his mate among the Alaskan Tigers was unexpected. He always wanted a female bear as his sow mate, and to raise a few cubs of his own. What he didn't need was a tigress with trust issues.

*A love that could destroy them...*

Finding his mate should be the best day of Thorben's life, but when he comes to Taber's aid and discovers his destined tigress mate is already his brother's mate, brotherhood must overcome nature, because bears mate for life.

# Chapter One

Taber Brown rubbed his eyes with the back of his hand for the umpteenth time in the last twenty minutes. Hour after hour, they scanned every shred of evidence Adam's team brought back from San Francisco once they seized Victor. They hoped to discover something that would lead them to Pierce, but nothing so far. Everything they discovered reinforced their belief—Victor only teamed with Pierce to further his own agenda.

Could Pierce be so daft he wouldn't have seen Victor's true motivation? That was the question haunting not only Taber, but the Elders of the Alaskan Tigers as well. If they could see through Victor, surely Pierce had as well.

The papers cluttering the table detailed Victor's plans to bring Bratva—the brotherhood, a Russian shifter terrorist group—to the states. Over the years, it appeared Victor had been gathering followers from different shifter groups with like-minded beliefs.

9

Taber pushed papers aside, searching for his squeeze bottle of honey buried somewhere under the clutter. With hours left, before the day's end, he needed his honey to see him through. *Where did that damn bottle go?*

"Bear." Adam growled when Taber shoved more papers out of the way. "You finished your honey an hour ago."

"Shit."

"We stocked some for you in the compound's kitchen. Go get a refill and then get some damn sleep. You're grumpy when you're tired."

"I'm a bear, damn it." He rose, stretching his long legs. To him being a bear explained everything, but to the tigers well it might have been another story, especially after Adam raised an eyebrow. At that moment, Taber didn't care.

He'd swing by the kitchen for another bottle of honey before checking in with the men guarding Victor. He also hoped to find Ty or Raja before hitting the sack, to see if any progress was made gaining information from Victor.

The kitchen was on the far side of the main compound building, away from the private quarters of the Alpha and Lieutenant, giving them both seclusion and security. He slipped his hand into the front pocket of his sweatshirt, his fingers wrapping around his cell phone. As he turned the last corner, leading to the long hallway toward the kitchen, he collided with a woman.

"Shit," she said. Coffee covered the front of her shirt.

"I'm sorry. I didn't expect anyone to be around here this time of the night." Being nearly seven foot, he stared down at her. The white stripes sprinkled through her long, curly brown hair caught his attention. *Did she do those on purpose?* According to his cousin, they were highlights, but Taber couldn't fathom why anyone would want such stripes painting their hair.

"You're a damn shifter. You should have sensed me coming!" She growled at him, blotting the coffee stain with a napkin, but it only served to make matters worse.

"I said I was sorry, what more do you want woman?"

"Obviously nothing." She snarled, shoving the napkins in her nearly empty coffee cup. She released a heavy sigh and moved to pass him.

He reached out, wrapping his hand around her small arm. She winced as if expecting him to cause her pain. He hated seeing fear resonating in her eyes. *What happened to cause her such distress?* "You're right, I should have sensed you, but I wasn't paying attention. Let me get you another cup."

A sudden shot of electricity vibrated through their contact. He couldn't tear his gaze from her.

*This can't be happening. My mate can't be a tigress. I won't have it. Especially a tigress with haunting in her eyes.*

"So you can spill it over me again? I think not." She pulled her arm free and pushed past him. He turned, his gaze following her as she sauntered down the hallway away from him. The sway of her hips drew his attention to her long, lush legs. The three-inch high heels she wore only served to add more sashay to her swaying hips. He wanted to run after her, to explore the electric jolt he received from her contact, but he instructed his feet to remain where he stood. He didn't want a tigress as his mate, and he doubted he could help ease the pain within her eyes.

\* \* \*

Unwilling to go back to the kitchen for another cup of coffee, Kallie walked across the compound back to her room. The cold night air sent shivers down her spine, thankfully it wasn't snowing again. She loved winter and all the white, fluffy snow, but they had more than enough the last few days to satisfy her need.

*Damn, bear. Who the hell does he think he is, laying a hand on me?* A simple touch served to remind her of all the years she suffered at the hands of another. She did her best to block the haunting memories and thanks to Adam's appearance she managed to keep them at bay again.

"Hey Kallie, what you doing out at this time of night?" Unlike with Taber, she now had her senses on high alert and smelled Adam before he stepped from the darkness. Heavy circles shadowed under his eyes and his shoulders sagged in defeat. *Whatever is going on is taking a toll on the lead guards.*

"I was grabbing a cup of coffee before my shift at command central." When Adam's gaze fell to her empty hands, she pointed to her solid sweater. "That damn bear wasn't paying attention and spilled it on me. I'm just going to change quickly."

"Tigers are quiet creatures, unlike bears. He probably didn't hear you coming."

"I guess." She glanced down at one of her favorite green sweaters and hoped the coffee would wash out. "I'll see you later. I have to change. Mark gets grumpy when I'm late."

"Be safe. You know we have a prisoner on the grounds."

She nodded and left to change. *Who is this prisoner?* Many in the compound assumed because of her job in command central she might have inside information, but in reality she was in the dark as everyone else. The Elders and their guards were tightlipped when it came to security issues, unless they were briefing the whole clan.

Her apartment was a studio at best, with a small kitchenette, sitting area, and a bed that dominated most of the room. Many of the unmarried guards lived in similar styled studios. The small space didn't bother the male guards since they rarely cooked, but she missed having a house and privacy without neighbors on each side. Every time she opened her door there was someone nearby. Since moving to Alaska, her clan had been building new cabins for the guards, and her name had nearly reached the top of the list. It wouldn't be much longer until she had a real home to call her own.

The only one benefit to her current living arrangement was that she didn't have to do the laundry. Twice a week some of the clan woman would come by to pick up her linens and clothes. They'd be returned later that day washed, and folded neatly on her bed. Doing laundry had never been high on Kallie's enjoyment list.

Slipping the soiled sweater off, she tossed it into the laundry bag, before grabbing another from the drawer. Another favorite sweater, a warm, heather grey with bright white stitching, and rosy pink trimming around the collar, waist, and sleeves.

If that bear came near her again she'd be sure to stay a good distance away, especially if she had anything to drink in her hands. She wouldn't tolerate him ruining another favorite sweater. This particular sweater gave her a confidence she didn't normally have, even helped her forget about those damn white streaks in her hair.

Changed, she headed back to command central, where she dreaded seeing Mark who would be irritated for cutting her arrival so close to shift change. She avoided stepping on any slick icy spots along the way. Yes, high-heeled, knee-high boots weren't best for this climate, but since finding the security of the Alaskan Tigers, she favored heels. For the first time, she could embrace being a woman and not just a tiger. She had heels to go with every outfit, for every occasion.

She opened the door and saw Mark pacing the room, his arms crossed over his chest. "Where have you been?"

"Mark, you're never going to find a mate if you keep barking at women. I thought you were a tiger, not one of those idiot wolves." He continued to glare at her, waiting for an answer to his question. "Come on, Mark, give me a break. That damn bear ran into me. He

14

spilled coffee on my sweater, so I had to change. Plus, I'm on time."
She flashed him a smile, hoping to warm his chilly heart.

"Fine." He grabbed his coat from the back of the chair, nodding
to the bank of computer screens. "You see any unannounced
movement in area four, contact Ty or Raja *privately* about the activity,
no matter the time. You understand?"

Her gaze moved to each computer monitor before returning to
Mark. "It's not my first day on the job, I can handle it." Would he
ever trust she could do the job even though she was a woman? She
doubted it, but what mattered was Ty and Raja thought she could. "Is
that where the prisoner is being held?"

"How…" He frowned.

"I ran into Adam on my way to change, he mentioned there was
a prisoner on the grounds. So, is that where he is?" She glanced to
area four to be certain there was no change in activity. She'd have to
watch that section very carefully while on duty. They wouldn't have a
prisoner in their compound, especially not one of their own, unless it
had something to do with the rogue gang they had been tracking.

He stepped toward the door, his dark shadowed eyes indicating
he was clearly ready for his shift to end and to get some sleep. "Yes,
now be sure to pay close attention to the monitors."

"I got it." She saluted as he closed the door.

*Peace.* She sank onto the chair, her gaze scrolling over the
monitors and then returning to area four again. *Who do they have in that
old abandoned cabin?* It couldn't be Pierce, the leader of the rogues.

There was no way Ty or Raja would stand for him to be that close to their mates, not after he single-handedly killed Tabitha's and then Bethany's parents, and nearly killed Bethany when she was kidnapped and used as ransom to gain Tabitha. To her Alpha and Lieutenant, whatever information could be gained would never outweigh the risk to their mates. They were good men and would protect not only their mates, but the whole clan, regardless of the danger to themselves.

Movement in area three caught her eye, drawing her attention from area four for a brief moment. *Taber.*

Her core moistened with desire just watching him stroll across the grounds. Ever since their encounter earlier, her body longed for his touch, to feel his fingers running over her skin. It had been too long since she had the touch of another, but then she remembered why.

*Betrayal.*

Only once had she given her heart and body to another, and in the end it nearly killed her. She vowed to never make that mistake again, and she'd be damn certain she wouldn't with a bear. Filthy creatures.

# **Chapter Two**

Honey in hand and one in his sweatshirt pocket for later, Taber crossed the grounds, determined to check on the progress of their prisoner before crashing for the night.

He swallowed a squeeze of honey and then using his forefinger, he pressed the button on his ear to transmit a signal to the guards, as well as command central. "Taber, area four."

His ear piece crackled. "Approved."

It was *her* voice! That woman—his destined mate, he spilled coffee on. Even with a hint of anger lacing her words as she yelled at him earlier for staining her sweater, she sounded like an angel to Taber.

*Too bad, she's a freaking tigress.*

He had nothing against tigers. He considered the Alaskan Tigers part of his family or he wouldn't be helping them with their fight against the rogues. Though, he'd rather be home in Nome catching salmon in his stream and searching for a sow mate of his own. Not a tigress…

He shook his head, pushing her from his thoughts, before opening the cabin door. The West Virginia Alpha, Jinx, leaned against the wall with his cowboy hat riding low on his head, effectively shielding his eyes from view. Next to Jinx, Korbin stood guard, his body stiff and arms crossed behind him—ready for action.

"How's it going?" Taber shut the door behind him.

"He's not giving anything up yet. Raja just sedated him for the night. Everyone needs rest. Ty and Raja selected Korbin and a couple other guards to take watch," Jinx explained.

Raja exited the adjoining room. "I thought you would have turned in."

Taber waved the bottle of honey. "Honey run and I thought I'd check the progress before I did."

"Jinx, you mind waiting until Thomas gets out here?" When Jinx nodded, Raja turned back to Taber. "Come on, I'll fill you in on the way."

They stepped out into the cold night air. Snowflakes dotted the air, landing in Taber's hair and on his cheeks. Before long, the snow now coating the ground would be covered with another fresh layer. Not that it bothered Taber. He lived in Alaska for the cold weather. Snowy terrain was second nature to his kind, and with the snow forcing humans inside they didn't have to worry about prying eyes catching them when they shifted.

"Victor's not giving anything up. He doesn't believe we have any leads. Connor was able to add a few red flags to Victor Senior's passport, so he didn't make it through customs, and is now on his way back to Russia." Raja stared into the night's sky for a moment. "Being the head of the shifter terrorist group in Russia isn't going to stop him from trying to get back in the states if he wants, especially if he suspects someone is onto him. He would have the same connections we have, and could remove those red flags without too much hassle."

"If he's not telling us anything, what now? Want me to take a crack at him?"

"Not yet. Ty and I will go at him in the morning. If he still doesn't give us the information we need, we'll find other means of making him talk, but we have to be quick. The longer he's here, the more dangerous it is for the clan."

Taber knew Raja was concerned about Tabitha and Bethany. The original plan had been to detain Victor somewhere outside the compound, away from the mates, woman, and children. "We'll keep them safe." Taber hoped to relive Raja's concerns. "We've already doubled the guards on duty." Taber sighed when they neared the warmth of Raja's quarters, his body screamed with exhaustion.

Raja nodded and waved Taber inside. "Get some rest. We'll deal with Victor tomorrow, when we're both refreshed from a night's rest."

Taber caught sight of the tiger's mate, Bethany, asleep on the sofa. She must have been waiting for Raja. Shadow and Styx, her guards, sat nearby. Taber tapped Raja's shoulder and headed to the guest room. He was ready to collapse into bed and catch as much sleep as he could in the few short downtime hours he had. But sleep proved elusive. Thoughts of Kallie crept into his mind, the memory of her sexy voice hardened his shaft instantly. *If only she wasn't a tigress.*

* * *

After hours of tossing in bed, Taber gave up on sleep. His hard shaft and body demanded he go to Kallie. Rising, he stretched and rolled his head from side to side. He needed coffee and more honey to lift the fog from his brain.

Not wanting to wake Raja and his mate, he quietly stepped to the counter and made a pot of coffee. While the coffee perked, he stood by the counter looking out the window at the snow covered grounds. A thin layer of white powder lay on top of what had fallen yesterday. Before long spring would be upon them and the snow would melt. Alaskans didn't have summers like the continental United States. Winter being the main season here, there was no need for air conditioners. To Taber the colder air made the land even more special—a place he never wanted to leave. This was his home.

The communication device, still in his ear, pierced his hearing. "The activity level is increasing in area four. I can't raise the guards on their communication device. Nearest Elder or Elder team member report to area four and advise on the situation." Kallie's voice was sharp and held a note of concern.

"Taber, reporting to area four." He shut off the coffee and ran steady to the door, no longer worrying if he woke Raja and Bethany.

"Raja, reporting as well. Contact Shadow and have her report to duty."

"Yes, sir." Kallie responded to Raja through the transmitting system, and then added Shadow to the conversation, explaining the situation. The urgency in her voice tugged at Taber, but his need was trumped by the threat hanging in the air.

Taber fought the temptation to shift. He was faster in bear form, but with no idea of what awaited them, he had to preserve his energy and keep his weapons intact. He normally didn't carry a gun, but with Victor on site and the danger level spiking with each minute their prisoner drew breath, all guards who knew how to shoot were equipped with weapons. Tranquilizer guns were also stored throughout the compound, within quick reach if the situation became out of control.

Taber skidded to a halt as Thomas stumbled out of the cabin where Victor was being held. Thomas' face was pale and blood dripped from his nose.

"What the hell happened?" Taber held a breath.

"Victor somehow broke through one of the chains. I thought he was still passed out, and I was checking on him when he attacked."

Thomas slipped off his shirt and used it to soak up some of the blood. "He only had one arm free, but he packs a damn punch."

Taber whipped around him and into the cabin. Korbin was already there, adding more chains to secure the now sedated Victor. Raja entered on Taber's heels.

"I told Thomas to shift and go to a healer. Marcus is on his way, he'll take over Thomas' duty. We need to deal with Victor today. We got lucky this time, next time we might not." Raja glanced from the prisoner to Taber. "Ty's gathering the team and we'll need a plan of action before we take on Victor. I'm tired of putting the clan at risk. We'll gather the information from Victor one way or another and then…"

Raja didn't say more. Everyone in the room knew once they had the information they needed from Victor, he was a dead man. They couldn't allow Victor to roam free again as a rogue. There were no alternatives. Being a shifter meant no weakness, especially not one in a position of power, like Raja and Ty.

# Chapter Three

Taber sat on one of the leather chairs surrounding the conference table. The weeks of only a few hours of sleep had begun to take its toll on not only him but everyone in the room. Even dividing their resources to have someone working through the extensive information and potential leads night and day, still meant longer hours for him and the Elders. He knew he couldn't continue down this path of little to no sleep night after night if he was to be ready for an attack. Rest was a must.

The Elders of the Alaskan Tigers clan, Ty, Tabitha, Raja, and Bethany, sat at the head of the table, the weight of the situation clearly visible in their eyes. The Captain of their Guards, Felix and Shadow, stood on each side of Elders as they always were. Ty and Raja not only had the clan to think about, but also their mates, and Tabitha had the imposing duty to not only the Alaskan Tigers, but to all tiger shifters. Without her they would cease to exist. She was the Queen of all Tigers.

Though Taber was a Kodiak bear shifter, it didn't mean he would not be affected if she did not carry out her duty. The Alaskan Tigers and the Kodiak Bears had worked together to bring peace to the region's shifter population. Without Ty and his clan, Alaska would still be in turmoil. Rumor and lore suggested once Tabitha united all tiger shifters, other shifters, and other species, they would band together and there'd be harmony amongst all.

Taber was here not only to repay a debt, but because he valued their friendship. Their fight was his fight, just as he knew he could count on them if things were reversed. Victor was a threat to all shifters. Victor and his father planned to bring Bratva to the states. If that happened, all shifters would be in danger.

"Now that everyone has had their coffee and the fog is lifting from your brains, we can begin." Ty waved a hand for everyone to be seated. "Regardless of our attempts, Victor has been uncooperative. He keeps repeating *the end will be coming for you. Long live Bratva.* We know who Bratva is, but the members, besides Victor Senior, are unknown. Connor and Lukas are heading the intelligence team, so if anyone can find the information it's them." Ty turned to Connor. "Do you have anything to report at this time?"

"Only that the Bratva is very dangerous. They control all Russian shifters, no matter the species. If you don't conform to their ways, they'll send a message by killing someone you love. If all else fails, they won't hesitate to kill to maintain order. Humans and shifters live in fear of their organization. The Russian citizens only know them as a terrorist group. They don't realize the Bratva are shifters. Humans are collateral damage to them. They could care less if any humans were injured or killed because of their actions." Connor placed a picture on the main screen. "This is Victor Senior. The information I gathered leads me to determine his animal has taken over and there's nothing left to the person who once was."

"There must be something we can do…to save the Russian shifters?" Bethany stared at Raja.

"Do *you* want to go to Russia?" Adam lowered is head. "I apologize. I spoke out of line. I only mean that it's unlikely anyone would volunteer to go, and if the Russian shifters are under Bratva's control already, there's little we can do."

"No, we can do something," Raja said. "Taking Victor Senior out of his position of power might be enough to halt the organization and free the shifters under its control."

"And how do you plan to do this?" Taber stepped forward.

"A trap. How else?" Raja raised an eyebrow. "You know the kitty within all of us loves to draw people in. We'll dangle a string and he'll come running, that string being his son."

"You want to bring him to the states? Isn't that what we've been trying to avoid, why we took Victor down before Victor Senior could arrive?" Adam frowned.

Ty stood at the head of the table. "We don't want him here, and he'd realize it's a trap. Nevertheless, with any luck we'll be able to find out more of his plans. We have too much to deal with already.

The Russian shifters need to free themselves from his hold if they're going to survive. We'll keep a close tab on Bratva and if his followers become a problem for us, they'll be dealt with."

"What's this trap that will help take Victor Senior out of his position within Bratva?" Marcus, Raja's brother-in-law, asked.

"We'll send him a video like Pierce sent us when he kidnapped Bethany."

Taber noticed Raja didn't mention the other video, the one where Pierce killed Bethany's family. Everyone in the room was probably already thinking about it. The sadness around Bethany's eyes and frown engraved on her forehead were clear indications where her thoughts laid.

Ty continued. "Let Victor Senior know we have his son, and if he wants him back, he'll have to come for him. If he comes, which is doubtful, there's our chance. We'll offer him a deal, his son's life in exchange for information *and* that he step down from his current position."

"After all this, we're going to let Victor live?" Marcus leaned forward, placing his hands on the table, his energy vibrating off the table. Marcus was the only other mated male in the room besides the Elders, and he wasn't just thinking of the clan, but also of his wife Tora, Raja's sister.

"No, Victor is too much of a threat to us, other shifters, and humans. He's a rogue and he'll die, no matter the outcome with Victor Senior. Like I said, it's just a string we're dangling, playing our cards to win." Ty stalked the room like a caged tiger. "Back to Victor, Tabitha has a way to get him to release any information he might be withholding."

Tabitha placed her coffee mug on the table, her gaze sweeping across the room. "Everyone who sits before me knows of the book that will help guide me in uniting the tiger shifters. It has let me know about the healer, Galan who has recently joined our clan, and many other things. The book has provided us a way to gather what we need." She pulled a small vial from her pocket, holding it between her thumb and forefinger. "This will give us everything we need."

"How?" Adam leaned forward, his attention on the bottle in her hand. "If you're supposed to make him drink it, that's going to be difficult, he hasn't touched anything we've offered him."

"He doesn't drink it. I do." She sat the vial on the table.

"I'm not sure this is a good idea." Taber's voice broke the silence. "We can't risk you, Tabitha."

"I already had that argument with her." Ty leaned against the wall looking from his mate to Taber. "It gets worse," Ty said. "Go ahead, Tabby, tell them everything."

"Once I drink the liquid, I'll be able to see everything Victor won't tell us. I'll have full access to his mind, his memories, everything." She lifted her coffee cup, taking a sip before she continued. "I will have the information we need."

"How?" Felix, the Captain of Tabitha's Guards spoke up.

"With a touch…"

"There has to be another way!" Taber cut off Tabitha's explanation, glancing from Tabitha to her mate, Ty.

Tabitha nodded, acknowledging Taber's concern for her safety. "We're running out of time. The longer Victor's here the more danger for everyone. We need to worry about everyone's safety not just mine. He's restrained…"

"My Queen, this is too much danger. He broke free from his chain only hours ago." Felix turned to Ty. "How can you support this?"

"Felix, I understand your concern," Ty responded. "It's your duty to protect her, but the guardians of the book wouldn't put her in danger if there was another way. They wouldn't give us a guide to the information if it meant her death." Ty pushed away from the wall and walked toward Tabitha. "I'm not happy about this anymore than the rest of you. Tabitha is my mate, and more than anyone, I want her safe, but there's no alternative. The room will be full of guards, and Galan and Bethany will be standing by to heal in case anyone is injured." He touched his mate's shoulder. "Like Tabby said, the longer he's here the more danger the clan is in. We need to eliminate one threat so we can focus on Pierce. The longer we wait to take the gang of rogues down, the harder it will become."

Raja rose from his seat. "Ty, our mates, and I will come up with the best strategy for this plan. Once we have the final details the guards will be notified. In the meantime, we need your help in finding Pierce. He's our main concern if we're going to keep our clan safe. I want everyone to focus on locating him, and finding Robin Zimmer. The book has advised us she's also a key to finding Pierce. Her late husband had dealings with Pierce and might have told her something. She may know where the rogues were held up. We have to find her before the rogues do." Raja nodded, his signal the meeting and further discussion was over.

Tigress for Two: Alaskan Tigers

# Chapter Four

Taber stopped by command central for another stack of intelligence that needed to be reviewed before making his way back to Raja's quarters. Catching Kallie's scent at command central, invaded his head with visions of her. The memory made his shaft hard. *Damn fate for mating me with a tigress.*

Angry at his dumb fate luck, he had to blow off steam. He promised the beast within him a shift as soon as he read through the files. He'd let the bear free to roam in the icy stream running through the back of the compound, and if he was lucky he'd find dinner. In his bear form maybe Kallie wouldn't be so ever present in his mind.

"Hey, Taber." Raja pointed to a chair as Taber entered Raja's quarters. "We're about to get started, and we'd like you to join us."

Taber grew apprehensive. Why would Raja want him to sit in on the meeting when both sets of their guards were standing outside Raja's quarters? Taber knew Raja never acted without a reason, so he nodded, tossing the files on the coffee table and pulled a chair out at the kitchen table where the Elders sat. Taber glanced to Ty and Tabitha who were hand in hand at the end of the table. Taber still didn't like the idea of Tabitha risking her life to gather information from Victor. It wasn't a woman's place to confront danger head on. Women were precious and needed to be protected if their species was to continue, especially for the tiger shifters. Without Tabitha, they would simply cease to exist.

"What's on your mind, Taber?" Bethany asked when he continued to stare at Tabitha, his lips curved into a frown and the muscles in his shoulders tense with concern.

He shook his head, lowering his bulky frame onto the chair. "Nothing. This vial, how do you know it's safe?"

Tabitha released Ty's hand and placed hers on the book before her. It sprang open. "This book has been my guide since Ty came to Pennsylvania and found me in Pittsburgh. It's been the reason behind everything we've accomplished so far. Without it I wouldn't have thought to create the core group with Felix, Marcus, Thomas, and now Shadow. They're going to be key elements to our success. This book brought us our healer, Galan. Without him we might never have known about Bethany's ability to heal."

"Okay, but…"

"Let me finish, Taber, and I promise you'll soon understand." Tabitha paused a moment, waiting for his silence. "This book has been passed down from generation to generation in my family. There was a whole section hidden, lying in wait until it found me. Every time I need answers it's there, guiding me on the path I need to take to unite the tiger shifters. This newest development is just one of many. I have no fear this vial will do anything more or less than what it says and I'll come to no harm. It's our only option, and we're running out of time."

"I don't think it's worth the risk. Couldn't one of us take it instead? That way, you're safe. I could take it…" Taber reached for the bottle, only to have Tabitha's hand tightly clench around it.

"As her mate, don't you think I would have offered the same if it was a possibility?" Anger flared in Ty's eyes.

Taber retracted his hand as if bitten. "I meant no disrespect. I only wish to keep you both safe."

"We don't have time for this." Tabitha stared at the vial in her hand. "Only I can do it."

"Tabitha will do this for us, and we need to figure out how to keep her safe." Raja placed a tray on the table and began pouring the coffee. "After Victor broke his chains this morning, we doubled them, but we don't know if they will hold him. There's no way we can surround him since Tabitha will have to touch him. Where does that leave us? Packing the room full of guards armed to the max?"

"Only a few guards. If things get out of control, I don't want anyone hit by friendly fire. We can have more forces waiting in the other room with Bethany and Galan." Ty slid his arm around Tabitha's shoulders, pulling her to his body. "Felix, Adam, Taber,

Raja, and I will escort Tabitha. Shadow and Styx will protect Bethany so if there's chaos I want them to get her out of there."

Raja leaned back, grabbing his coffee cup. "Felix and Ty will get Tabitha to safety if things go wrong. We've already decided to put Victor down in a humane way. There's a tranquilizer gun loaded with the correct dose to stop his heart. Taber, you'll be in charge of that. I'd rather take him down with my bare hands." His voice was low, but in a room full of shifters, everyone heard him. Bethany, the only non-shifter, wrapped her hand around Raja's, squeezing it lightly. He brought her knuckles to his lips and kissed them softly. "Don't worry love, we'll protect you."

Taber watched the display of emotion with an uneasy feeling in the pit of his stomach. His gaze wandered to the left to find Ty and Tabitha embracing as well. He understood that shifters preferred to touch their mates, to put them at ease, but their intimate moment of affection made him feel very alone.

*Alone?* Bears preferred to be alone, but for the first time, Taber didn't. He wanted a mate, the same happiness that Ty and Raja had with their mates. *What I don't want is a tigress mate. Why can't I settle down with a sow, and raise a few cubs?*

# Chapter Five

Taber thumbed through yet another file, his eyes crossing after reviewing one computer printout after another, while Raja and Styx filmed Victor. Connor would place a sound over, before they sent the final recording to Victor Senior. Everyone was on standby waiting for the recording to be sent before Tabitha could find the answers they need, because once they had the information from Victor there would be no reason to keep him alive.

"Taber, why don't you take a break? You and the others have been at those files nonstop for days." Bethany handed him another bottle of honey to replace the one he just finished.

"Thank you." He took the bottle of honey and squirted the golden liquid in his mouth. As he swallowed, the tension melted from his body. "That's exactly what I needed. I'm fine now."

"You're working too hard." Bethany stretched on the sofa across from him, her own stack of files on her lap.

"Isn't that like the pot calling the kettle black?" He raised an eyebrow. "You've been putting in just as many hours as the rest of us, and I suspect getting less sleep. Yet you're sitting there doing the same thing I am."

"That's different."

"How?" Interested in her excuse, he put the pages he was reading down on the table.

"Ummm...I'm...the Lieutenant's mate. I have to pull my weight somehow."

"Bethany, I'll give you credit, you're quick on your feet and that's almost a believable excuse, too." He chuckled. "I know how much you want to take down Pierce. We all do. We can't stop now. The next lead might be the break we need to take down his gang of rogues."

A knock on the door sent Taber on high alert. Nerves on edge, he shot Shadow a quick glance before advancing to the door. No one should be here, not at this time, without warning. Someone couldn't have gained access to the compound without alerting security, but until he knew who was standing on the other side of the door it was his responsibility to protect Bethany. As he crept to the door, Taber tilted his neck from side to side, loosening his tight muscles. Taber nodded to Shadow, a signal to be ready for anything.

A familiar scent wafted past his nose just a step from the door. His shoulders eased. The person waiting for him to answer the door posed them no harm. *Kallie...*

He pulled open the door and the sweet smell of morning, where the dew still clung to the ground and summer just around the corner—pure Kallie—hit him with such force he almost took a step back. His body called to her. He wanted to take her in his arms and hold her against his body. If she wasn't a different species, he would have. He would have forgotten about all the danger and claimed his mate. *Damn it!*

"What is it, Kallie?" Taber had to get out of sight before his hard shaft became noticeable. Out of sight, out of mind wasn't really the case when it came to mating, but it eased the longing, at least until he claimed her.

"There's a development, I need to find Raja or Ty. I checked Ty's quarters, but there was no answer. Do you know where the Elders are?"

His gaze traveled over her face, taking in the fear that burned in her eyes and the strain of her clenched teeth. He longed to reach out and touch her, soothe away her anxiety. "Shadow, stay with Bethany. I'm going to take Kallie to Raja." Without waiting for an answer, he slipped out the door, closing it behind him. His attention focused on Kallie. "What's going on?"

"I think I should tell my Elders first."

He gently grabbed her arm when she started to scurry down the hall, her high heel boots clicking on the hardwood floor. "Answer me this, is there immediate danger that I shouldn't leave Bethany and Shadow alone? Do I need to order more guards?"

"Not immediate, no. Now let's go." She jerked her arm free of his grasp.

He followed her down the hall, watching the way her ass swayed in the tight, faded blue jeans. His beast clawed within him, demanding her, but he refused. *I need to get out of here and back to Nome before I can no longer keep the beast chained up.*

His twin, Thorben, would see that Taber never heard the last of it when he found out Taber's mate was a tigress. Thorben didn't have the same open views as Taber did when it came to other shifters. His twin believed the bear shifters should stay in Nome and mind their own business. Their family hadn't been able to maintain control over the bear shifters of Alaska and the Alaskan Tigers had to step in, injuring his twin's pride. It was the only thing the brothers disagreed on.

Taber and Kallie stepped out into the cool afternoon air. The shining sun against the snow cast a shimmering glitter over the land. The ground was slick from the snow melting and refreezing, and when Kallie's high heel boot walked on the ice she nearly fell flat on her ass. If Taber hadn't hooked his arm around her waist she would have done just that.

"Careful." He helped her regain balance, but the damage was already done. The electric current that told shifters they were to be mated, traveled between them. Their gazes met. It did not go unnoticed by her because her eyes revealed the shock. History claimed, once a connection was made there was no chance in breaking the bond formed, linking them. *Damn it!*

"It can't be." She pulled from his grasp with such force she nearly slipped and collapsed to the ground. When he reached out to steady her, she jerked back as if she'd been burned. "Don't touch me. I don't want or need a mate, especially not a bear."

"Listen woman, I'm not happy about this either. I want a sow and cubs of my own." He stepped aside. "Maybe there's something we can do about this...to get out of the bond."

"Yeah, stay away from me."

Raja and Styx appeared from the side of the building. "What's going on?" Raja frowned.

"Kallie has information she feels the Elders need to know." Taber was thankful for the reprieve from Kallie before his temper flared beyond his control. "I'll leave you to talk."

"Taber stay, we'll go into the conference room and continue this conversation." Raja opened the door and led the way.

* * *

Taber sat on one of the leather chairs, eager to get this over with and away from Kallie. For someone who was only a member of the Alaskan Tigers, and not an Elder or guard, Taber had seen a lot of her since spilling coffee on her.

"So what's this information you bring?" Raja leaned against the wall, hands in the pockets of his stonewashed jeans. Styx might be

Shadow's second when guarding Bethany, but he hung back close to the door, guarding Raja.

Kallie sat, clearly uncomfortable to be in front of the Elder and guards, her gaze traveling between Raja and Styx, before finally settling on Raja. "The guards you have stationed above the compound are reporting activity among Pierce's men. It seems as though they're preparing for something. I fear from the information I've received, they might be planning an attack."

Her statement got everyone's quick attention as silence filled the room.

"Styx, find Ty and tell him what's going on. Get Tabitha and Bethany together and stay with them." Raja moved to peer out the conference room windows, not that he could see much beyond the trees. The compound area had been picked for its isolation. The undeveloped land surrounding the compound gave them even more privacy. Ty and Raja purchased all the surrounding tracts when they built the small town to ensure no one would infringe on their clan, and that they could expand, as needed.

"Raja, I think we should proceed with the plan, as soon as possible," Taber said. It was time to let Tabitha work her magic on Victor. If there was going to be attack on the compound they needed to deal with Victor and eliminate him as a threat. They couldn't afford to have someone help him escape while they were defending their land and clan.

Raja nodded. "I agree. Kallie go back to command central. Work with Mark to find out anything else."

Ty walked into the room, his green dress shirt hanging open. He spared Kallie a brief look as she left and then focused on Raja. "Tabby's with Bethany and the guards, but she's ready. Has the video been sent to Victor Senior yet?"

"I was on my way to deliver it to Connor when Taber and Kallie found me. I think we should send it first."

Ty fastened the last button on his shirt. "You do that. I'll meet up with the women and guards, and we'll meet you in section four. Taber, if you could head over to command central and see if there's new information. You have twenty minutes and then I want you to meet us in section four to help guard Tabitha."

Taber rose from the chair. "Whatever you need." He followed Ty out of the conference room, and then headed in the opposite direction, following Kallie's trail. She left behind a scent that was burned in his brain.

\* \* \*

Heading back to command central, Kallie cursed her luck for running into Taber again. The one man in the whole compound she wanted to stay away from yet it seemed as if fate kept throwing them together. When she went to Raja's quarters she expected to find Shadow, Styx, or even one of the other guards. She definitely didn't expect to see Taber. It never crossed her mind that space was limited with the Captains of the Guards, each occupying one of the guest

41

rooms in the main compound along with Raja's sister Tora and her family in another It made sense for them to be close with danger lurking the clan, especially with a prisoner close by. She expected Taber to have been in one of the cabins, not Raja's quarters.

She pushed Taber from her thoughts, at least the best she could, and opened the door. Mark sat behind the main station, watching the computer screens. His eyes appeared more drawn and worried than normal as he focused on one of the cameras covering an area of the undeveloped land surrounding the compound.

"Mark, anything happen while I was gone?" She slid into her post at the other desk. Kallie wasn't technically on duty, but even if Raja hadn't ordered her to help Mark, she couldn't leave him to watch all the screens with the impending danger.

"They've moved down the mountainside and found better coverage. It works to our advantage because though we can't see them, they can't see us either, not enough to attack. We have a team off to their south, watching. If they make a move we'll know. Did you find Ty?" He swiveled his chair around, cup of coffee in hand.

"I found Raja, but he sent one of the guards to get Ty. They seem to have something they need to do, but want to be kept advised on how the situation progresses." She glanced at Mark over her computer monitor. "Do you think they will attack?" Concern laced her voice like a well-worn shirt.

Mark didn't have a chance to answer before they heard someone lumbering up the steps. She met his eyes just as the door pushed open. Taber stood in the doorway. She kicked herself for not paying attention to the monitor. If she had been aware of Taber's arrival, she could have made an excuse for a coffee run.

"Taber, come in. What can we do for you?" Mark asked.

"Ty sent me for any new information received. I'd like to speak with the guards on the mountain. See what they know." The bear shut the door behind him and stepped into the small command central.

The hairs rose on the back of Kallie's neck. Taber's bulky frame seemed to take up most of the floor space. She couldn't breathe. She had to get out of here. With her haunted past running fresh through her mind, being closed in was more than she could take. "Mark, I gotta…" She bolted for the door, unable to finish the sentence.

Gulping the fresh cold air, she fought the nightmares that plagued her day and night.

# Chapter Six

Taber shook his head, completely confused by Kallie's sudden departure. He knew she didn't want this mating any more than he did, but wasn't her reaction a little overdramatic? He rolled his eyes and turned his attention to Mark, ready to get down to business. If he could help it, he didn't want anyone to know about their mating bond.

"Don't worry about Kallie, she's had a tough past. Closed spaces send her right into panic mode. She'll return once she gets her shit together." Mark swiveled his chair around to the computer monitors. "Kallie picked up a transmission from the guards shortly before I came to replace her. It's recorded. Let me call up the file and you can have a listen."

While Mark typed away on the keyboard, Taber's thoughts drifted back to Kallie. *Tough past?* He wondered what happened to her and if those white streaks in her hair were part of her haunted past.

"Here you are." Mark clicked another button.

45

A male voice crackled through the recording. "They've moved approximately twenty yards down the mountainside. We overheard that they're waiting for orders."

Kallie's voice was next. "I've located them, but they're semi-hidden from the camera. I can't get a good lock on them. Orders for what? Team one can you see what they're doing?"

Her voice held a hint of panic, but after seeing Mark's blank expression, Taber knew he was the only one to pick up on it. He continued to listen to the recording.

"We've got a read on them. They seem to be practicing hand-to-hand combat. No official data on what orders, but I would speculate they're planning an attack. Do you have a lock on the other threats?"

"All other threats accounted for…" Kallie's words were cut off by the guard.

"One of my men overheard they're waiting for Pierce's signal! Have you located him? Is he here?" The guard's voice was anxious. Taber suspected the guard was scanning the mountainside for the leader of the rogues.

"Negative. There's been no indication he's been here. I'll alert the Elders. Keep us advised of the situation on your end."

Mark turned the communication off. "That's the complete recording." He turned to Taber. "Do you think Pierce is here?"

"No, he's not stupid enough to risk being found. Attacking the compound is a death sentence and even with his beast controlling him, he knows he doesn't have a chance. He'll risk his followers, but

46

not himself." Taber glanced at the monitors. "Do you have the locations of the threats? Of the closest one?"

Mark stood and waved a hand at the map on the wall. "The pins represent each of the known threats and their last recorded location. The guards report in hourly unless there's movement. This is the closest one." He pointed to the red pin. The location was halfway up the mountainside, but they would have to go around to attack, otherwise with the steep jagged drop not even a shifter would survive.

"Okay. Ty and Raja are going to be busy, so if there is any movement or any other information coming in I want to know. If they are preparing to attack then obviously alert the Elders as well."

Taber's ear bud clicked to life with Ty's voice. "A group of us are heading to section four."

"I'm on my way as well," Taber replied and then turned back to Mark. "I want you and Kallie both on duty watching this situation until we're finished in section four. If there's even the slightest change, notify me immediately."

"Understood. I'll have one of the ground guards find Kallie."

"Very well." Taber walked to the door in two short strides. He needed to hurry. They were working on borrowed time, and had to get whatever information they could from Victor to dispel the threat.

Outside he found Kallie leaning against the rail, her earlier pink cheeks now a pale white. "Kallie." There were so many things he wanted to say, but it wasn't the right time. "Mark needs you inside."

The breeze blew her wild curls. For a moment she appeared angelic. Taber wanted to wrap her in his arms and keep her safe from whatever the coming hours might hold. Regardless of her troubled past, he could never see her as anything but innocent, and innocents needed to be protected.

* * *

Kallie released a sigh when Taber left. His spicy male aroma mixed with subtle traces of honey, was as a constant reminder that fate had paired her with a bear. She inhaled another deep breath of fresh air and exhaled, releasing the memories of the past.

# Chapter Seven

Taber met the other guards outside the cabin where Victor was being held. "We set then?" He checked the tranquilizer gun to make sure it was loaded with the right dose to exterminate Victor.

"Once Raja gets here. He's waiting for Conner to send the video." Ty turned to address everyone, his arm tightly around his mate's waist. "Remember, Felix, Adam, Taber, Raja, and I will go in with Tabitha. Shadow and Styx, you're in charge of protecting Bethany. Get her out of here if there's any danger. Galen, you leave with Bethany if there are any issues. With the first hint of danger, I want the rest of you to storm the room. Victor's life will end today."

"Just give me time to get what I need before you kill him," Tabitha said.

Raja ran toward them and skidded to a halt, his breathing heavy. "It's been sent. Let's get this done."

"Taber you go first, your bulk is more intimidating." Ty turned to Jinx. "You're in charge of the other guards. Remember Tabitha needs to get the information, but if the danger is too great, you know what to do."

Taber took the lead. He nodded for the guards to step into the adjoining room where the rest of the team waited. He checked the chains securing Victor to the chair. After he'd broken the last chain, the guards added another chain to the collar around his neck, preventing him from shifting. It was attached to the wall and wouldn't stop him if he broke through the other chains, but it would slow him down long enough to get the Elders and their mates out of harm's way.

* * *

Tabitha drank the vial while Taber double checked the chains. Felix and Adam fanned around Victor, leaving Ty and Tabitha in the middle between Taber, Felix, and Adam. Ty held his mate's hand as if afraid to let her go. He brought her hand to his lips and gently kissed her knuckles. "Be safe, but quick, my love."

"You worry too much." She nodded, an indication she was ready to get started. Slipping her hand from Ty's, she approached the sedated Victor. His sedation wouldn't block her from finding the information they needed, and it was safer with him unable to resist her. Taber knew her trust laid with the men protecting her. He valued the courage she shown as she neared the prisoner. She placed two fingers on each side of Victor's temple, obviously seeking connection to his thoughts and memories. A small light tipped her fingers as a connection flared to life. Victor stirred under her fingertips.

50

Taber held his breath. The sedation wouldn't last long. Tabitha had to make the most of the time she had. She closed her eyes and her body stilled with concentration. The room knew of her need for justice for her parents and Bethany's family. Though she probably wanted Victor's death to be painful, Taber was impressed with the focused she put into every move she made, reinforcing her courage.

"Tell me about Pierce." She inquired.

With her eyes closed, Tabitha spoke almost as if in a trance, describing what she saw. "Victor is in a room, packing. He must be preparing for his trip to San Francisco. It's dark, but there are city lights shining through the curtains. Pierce's rage is nearly out of control as he paces the room, screaming."

*"Go to San Francisco, visit with your family, while I do all the hard work. Find Robin, prepare to take down those ignorant tigers, and kill that bitch."* Tabitha's voice was rough and filled with hatred as she spoke Pierce's words, almost as if she was possessed.

Taber knew Pierce wanted nothing more than to kill her before she could unite the tiger shifters.

Her voice changed to a calm tone. *"You need to find Robin before someone else does. We know she left Virginia, traveling to Ohio, go follow her trail while her scent is still fresh. Stop bitching, you know I had this family thing long before you fucked up and killed that family in Virginia."*

Tabitha paused and inhaled a deep breath. When she spoke, her voice was her own. "We have to find Robin before they do. Pierce's anger over her slipping from under the cover of darkness is great, but

51

there's an evil in his eyes that tells me he'd rather torture her before killing her. He's enjoying the kills, and will kill again soon. He has to..." She stopped suddenly. "Wait, there's something else."

The room was an eerie silence.

"Tabitha, what are you seeing?" Ty probed.

"It's an email from his father." Tabitha's eyes rolled under her eyelids. "Bratva's members are already in the states, lying in wait. New York...there's a group there. He's thinking of Boston too, but his thoughts are too scattered, I can't figure out why. But Boston is important somehow. Victor never joined with Pierce because he was rogue, nor did he share his beliefs. He joined to find others for the Bratva, and he had. During his time with Pierce, he converted numerous members to his beliefs." Her arms began to shake as if the connection was draining her.

"It's not surprising Victor deceived Pierce the entire time. Rogues never seem to possess a sense of loyalty beyond themselves. Typically, it was that trait that prevented them from forming successful groups." Taber stated.

Tabitha continued. "Pierce is losing control of his followers. They were looking more and more to Victor. He never wanted to control the rogues, and Pierce's usefulness was running thin. Victor Senior was coming to the states to force his son to take full control over the rest of the rogues and eliminate Pierce. Victor was trying to do his father proud, to live up to his expectation, but no matter what he did it never seemed be to enough for his father."

52

# Chapter Eight

Taber watched Tabitha, unable to do anything but guard her. His tension rose as Victor stirred. He hoped they'd be able to get the job done before he surfaced from the drugs. Tabitha's body shook. She was beginning to falter with the connection taking much from her. He was about to suggest they end the process, until Kallie's voice filled his ear.

"Taber, you there?" He sensed dread in her tone.

"Go ahead, Kallie," he whispered, but didn't take his eyes off Victor and Tabitha.

"They're moving. They're coming straight for us. There's two teams. Ten threats. Shall I alert the guards?"

"Shit. Hold on." He turned to Ty, whispering to avoid disturbing Tabitha's concentration. "We've got to finish this *now*, they're coming."

"Tell Kallie to put out a call for all guards to report to their stations." Ty turned to Tabitha. "Tabitha, if you can hear me, we need you to end this. Danger is upon us. We have to get you to safety. Give me a signal if you understand."

Tabitha's eyes rolled, but nodded at Ty.

Taber shot Kallie a quick message. "Kallie, you and Mark stay put and lock the door. Don't come out, no matter what happens."

"Understood. Mark says we have ten minutes at most before they're on our doorstep."

Taber turned back to Ty. "We have less than ten minutes, we need to get the women to safety."

Tabitha broke the connection, standing on shaky legs as she reached for Ty. "They're his...they're coming for their leader."

Ty wrapped his arm around her waist. "What? Pierce isn't here."

"No, Victor's men. They've been under his charge the last few months. Pierce is losing control. Those are Victor's men in the hills." She leaned against Ty, weakened from the connection.

"Felix and Adam, get Tabitha and Bethany to the main compound. Shadow and Styx will go with you, and the other guards will meet you there." Ty kissed the top of Tabitha's forehead as Bethany entered the room. "Bethany, try your healing abilities on Tabby, help her regain her strength quickly so you guys can get to safety."

"You've got to go," Taber ordered. Victor's demise was approaching and even though Taber was ending Victor's life as humane as they could with the tranquilizer gun, the women didn't need to be present. "Go and see the women to safety. I'll terminate this problem."

"The guards will keep them safe. We'll stay and deal with whoever dares to attack our home." Raja took the gun from Taber's hand, as Felix rushed the women out of the room.

Victor's eyes fluttered open, finally surfacing from the drugs. Hatred, kindling like fire, heated his eyes as he strained against the chains. "They're coming for me. You'll never see tomorrow."

"That's where you're wrong. The few supporters you have will easily be disposed of, but it's you who won't see tomorrow." Raja raised the gun and shot Victor in the chest. His body shook as the lethal dosage took effect. His breathing grew ragged, and then he collapsed.

Taber stared at a lifeless Victor, and breathed a sigh of relief. Victor would never harm another. Their world would now be a little safer.

"Small victory for us, but Pierce is still out there, and we still have the rogues to deal with." Raja let the empty gun fall to the floor and stepped to the door. "Let's go kick some ass."

* * *

Kallie watched the men climb down the mountainside. She could do nothing to stop them, but keep the guards apprised of the rogues' progress. She slipped the small capsule that she kept around her neck between her fingers, enjoying its soothing coolness. It was the one insurance she had that she'd never again endure the same torture she had before. She'd never again be someone's pet, with no will of her own. She would die before that happened.

Today might be the day she had no other alternative than to use the capsule to take her own life, to end it all, but she prayed not. She reached into her desk drawer, grabbing the gun she stored there. *I won't go down alone.*

# Chapter Nine

Taber and the Elders had just stepped out of the cabin when Kallie's voice crackled in his ear piece.

"They're here."

He knew, from the way the guards around them were bracing for action, that she used the open communication so everyone with ear buds heard her warning. "I'd advise you, go to your mates." Taber said. "You're Elders, you need to be protected as well."

"That's not how we operate. When our clan is in trouble, we stand to defend it. Our women and children will be protected by all able male bodies…" Ty's words were cut off by gunshots at the main gate.

They ran to the gate, no one shifting yet. For security, they fought in their human forms, and would shift only if necessary, hiding their second nature as much as possible.

Taber ran past command central, hoping Kallie had taken his advice to stay safe.

The ground guards defended the main gate as a group of rogues attacked from the other side. "One got through. He broke free before I could detain him." Lance gave them a quick status update as they neared.

"Damn it." Taber frowned. "Kallie, do you have a mark on the threat?"

"Searching now," Kallie answered. "Shit! He's coming straight…" Her words where interrupted by the sound of a loud crash and a door splintering. Her scream filled his ear.

He turned to the Elders. "He's at command central."

"Ty go with Taber. I'll help here." Raja waved for them to leave.

"Do you think the rogue knew the layout and chose command central for a reason?" Taber ran even steps with Ty.

"How would they have found out about our layout?" Ty shook his head. "Damn it! It had to be Chris! He betrayed his own clan to assist Pierce when Tabitha first arrived in Alaska. He would have given the rogues the information to attack our compound, in order to save his sister. When we get through this fight, we'll send a team to Georgia to eliminate him. He won't get away with risking my mate and this clan again."

They slowed as they approached command center. The door lay in pieces on the floor, and a tiger's roar ripped through the air. Taber rushed past Ty, running full speed toward the door, hoping he wasn't too late to save Kallie.

Inside, Mark, in tiger form, was lying on the floor bleeding and unconscious. The rogue searched the monitors. Taber attacked, leaping in the air to pounce on the rogue and knock him to the floor. Wrapping a hand around the rogue's throat, Taber began squeezing the life from him. But the rogue wasn't shifting. Loosened his grip, he realized the rogue was human. "What do you want?"

"I was paid to lead the team. To find two women." The man's fingers clawed at Taber's hands around his neck.

"Who are you?" Ty glared at the man as he bent to check the pulse at Mark's neck. "And what have you done with the woman that was here?"

"My name is Kenneth. I was Special Forces until I found out about your kind. The woman…she took off." He pointed to the window. "I wouldn't have hurt her."

Ty raised an eyebrow. "Your actions don't speak very well, considering Mark's condition."

"He attacked me first. I know shifters can heal from gunshot wounds." He glanced back at Taber. "If you'd let me up, I'll explain why I'm here and maybe we can work this out. I didn't want to shoot him or anyone else."

"You've got another thing coming if you think I'm going to let you free. Talk, and then we'll decide what to do with you." Taber released the man's neck, but pushed him over and held both arms behind his back.

59

"I told you, I was hired to find two women. Sisters, taken against their will. If you check my jacket pocket there are pictures of these women."

Taber reached in and pulled out two photographs. *Kallie and Tabitha.* "What do you want with them? Who hired you?"

"Their husbands. They want their wives back."

Ty laughed. "Considering one of those women is my mate, I find your story hard to believe."

"The other woman is my mate." Taber's rage boiled in the pit of his stomach. He tightened his hold on the man's arms. *How dare he threaten what's mine?*

"These men had marriage licenses," Kenneth said.

"Those can be faked." Ty squatted over the man. "Who hired you?"

"Pierce and another man. I never met the second guy. He was out of town on business."

"You didn't find it odd that the man was doing business while his wife is missing?" Taber was tired of the games. This man couldn't be a stupid as he was trying to make believe. "Why did you take this job?"

Kenneth's eyes widened. "Yes, there were a number of questionable things about this job, but Pierce said the other man was trying to make reservations to return, but the flights were booked. I didn't think to question him. He had men ready, all I had to do was lead them." The man grimaced at the pain Taber inflicted when he tightened his grip. "Money! I did the job for the money. My sister's daughter has cancer. They need to pay her hospital bills. I did it for them. This one job allowed me to pay off their bills and cover the rest of her treatments."

With the human's blubbering confession, Taber released him and stripped away the soldier's weapons before he stood. "If you try anything, you'll regret it."

Kenneth lay on the floor, rubbing his neck and arms. "If I could see the women, to know the truth, I'll leave peacefully."

Taber stepped forward, pointing a gun to his face, ready to kill the man for the suggestion.

"Not going to happen. Do you think we're that stupid?" Ty laughed.

Raja entered the room, blocking the light from the entry. "He's human?"

"Special forces after Tabitha and Kallie," Taber explained.

"Why Kallie?"

"Supposedly they were kidnapped. That's all he knows. I don't understand how Kallie plays into all this." Ty leaned against the desk. "Where is she?"

"I haven't seen her. The situation outside has been dealt with. What should we do with him?" Raja paused next to Taber.

"We'll detain him in one of the cells, until we've made sure everyone's safe. Someone needs to find Kallie." Ty scanned the monitors. "I can't see her here. I think it's highly unlikely she went back to her room. She isn't one to leave her post. We'll get a tracker to find her."

"If you don't need me to deal with this rogue, I'll find Kallie." Taber wasn't one of the clan members who needed permission, but he sought Ty's consent out of respect.

"Go. Raja and I can handle the situation here. Contact me when you find Kallie. I want to know why she ran." Ty then turned to Raja. "Get the human in a cage. We need Galan to look at Mark."

Taber left to find Kallie. Once outside, he closed his eyes, leaning his head back to catch her scent. It didn't take long for him to get a fix on her, but her scent was different from the normal sweet smell of morning. It was strongly mixed with fear. His Kallie was terrified. Guided by his nose, the faster he ran as her scent grew stronger. *Maybe someone else got loose in the compound?* He sniffed the air, but didn't catch the scent of anyone else. Nothing unfamiliar and no one followed her.

He neared the back of the compound, closing in on the creek that only hours ago he promised his bear a rump. Her smell filled his senses. He turned around a corner and found her lying in the snow.

"What the hell?" He ran to her side, searching for any sign of injury. He found nothing. Her jeans and sweater were wet, but unstained with blood. She was unconscious.

Not caring about the snow, he dropped to his knees, wrapping her in his arms. A chain, she wore around her neck, slipped out from the collar of her sweater. The small capsule, which hung on the chain, was open. He took a deep breath, filling his lungs with her scent, and that's when he smelled it. Poison! Painless, but enough do the job.

"Damn it, Kallie, why?" He gently shook her body, trying to wake her, but she didn't stir. He checked her pulse. She was still breathing so it wasn't too late.

He stood and pressed his ear bud. "Taber here. I need a healer."

"Come to my quarters." Bethany's voice filled his ear.

"Hang in there, Kallie." He lifted her weak body in his arms and sprinted back the way he came.

*Damn it. I might not be thrilled to have a tigress as a mate, but I'll be damn if I let her die on me. Who gives a shit what Thorben thinks as long as Kallie and I are together.*

# Chapter Ten

Taber laid Kallie on a sofa, holding her hand and moving only far enough away to allow Bethany access. His head pounded. He hated being useless while his mate lay there dying.

"What happened?" Bethany knelt next to the sofa.

"Poison. I think she took it herself. Can you heal her?"

Bethany didn't answer. She slid Kallie's wet sweater up to her breasts and placed her hands on the bare flesh of Kallie's stomach. Closing her eyes, Bethany began to focus. "I can help her, but she's going to suffer. My healing will counteract the poison and then leave her ill for the next few hours. Unless Galen, can…"

Galen placed his hand on Bethany's shoulder "No, my healing would do the same. You're becoming a wonderful healer. Go ahead, I'll supervise."

Galen had been training Bethany's healing abilities since arriving in Alaska. She was picking up quickly, surprising everyone since she was human and up until a few weeks ago, didn't know she had any abilities.

"May I, Taber?" Bethany's green eyes glanced up at him, as if seeking his approval.

He frowned, completely baffled. "Why would I have a say in her well-being? She's one of your tigers."

"I feel she's your mate." She held up her hand when Taber started to shake his head. "Don't deny it. As a healer, I can feel the mating current running within a body. The mating process isn't complete yet, but it has started. You'll be mated."

He simply nodded. There was no time to waste debating that he and Kallie were too different to ever work. For years, he searched for his mate, and now that he found her, he wished he had stayed in Nome instead of coming when Ty called. Since literally running into Kallie, he always seemed to be on the wrong foot with her. She made him feel like a bear in a china shop, if he moved too much he might forfeit his hide.

Bethany began the healing process, her hands pressed roughly against Kallie's stomach. Kallie moaned in pain, but her eyelids remained closed. Her fingers curled around his in a death-grip when Bethany removed her hands from Kallie's stomach.

"Take her to her room and stay with her. The next few hours will be critical. Strip her of her wet clothes and use your body to warm her. She'll have extreme chills while her body works to repair the damage the poison did to her internal organs." Bethany stretched and rose from the sofa, grabbing the mug of tea that Tabby held out to her. She glanced back at Taber as he lifted Kallie in his arms. "If she isn't kept warm, her body won't heal…and she won't survive."

\* \* \*

Kallie was surprised to be alive, let alone naked in her room next to a very naked Taber. She squirmed, trying to scoot away from him, but his large arms trapped her against his chest. *What the hell? How did we get here?*

She closed her eyes, hoping to remember what happened and more importantly how she ended in bed with him. She couldn't remember anything except the attack. People attacked the compound, a man broke down command central door, she ran, and then held the capsule in her hand. After that, everything was blank.

"Hey, wake up!" Wanting answers, she pounded her fist against the barrel of his chest. He woke with a start and extended his claws. She winced as they pressed into her back.

"Taber." She whispered, trying not to spook the bear any more than he was.

"Damn it, Kal, you should know better than to abruptly wake a sleeping bear. I could have attacked you." He retracted his claws and pulled her to his body, snuggling her close to him as his eyelids drifted shut once again.

"Stop that." She swatted his arm, wriggling to get out of his grip.

"You need to stay here. My body heat…" His words were heavy with exhaustion.

"What the hell do you mean?"

"Kal, you tried to poison yourself. Bethany has done what she could to reverse it, and now your body needs to heal the damage. Stop moving so much. I'm on strict orders from the healers to provide body heat and keep you calm for the next forty-eight hours."

Her fingers roamed her neck, seeking the capsule she kept on a chain. She could feel by the weight alone, it was empty. She had one safety measure and it failed her. She left Mark, and jumped out the window, running until she was certain no one had followed her. Kallie then grasped the only escape she had been certain of. "You're dreaming if you think I'm going to stay cuddled with you for the next two days."

"I'll sedate you if I have to." He ran his hand over her arm, and she trembled with excitement. "Damn it woman, look at you. You're freezing. Your body can't provide the heat you need while it's doing such extensive repairs. Once the chills have past you won't need my heat and I can get out of your bed, but until then be still."

When she continued to fight him, he added. "The longer you fight me the longer you'll be stuck next to me. You're using energy that your body needs to heal."

She was cold and his body was so warm, like her own personal heater. Sucking up her pride, she curled around him.

"Why, Kallie?" He whispered, gently rubbing her arm.

"They were here for me." She cringed at the thought. They would find her and try to take her back. She knew it was inevitable, and tried to prepare for it, but her plan failed.

"Kenneth, he was the threat that attacked command center. He showed us a picture of the two women he was here to find. Tabitha and you. But what I don't understand is why. Why was he after you?" He squeezed her tight against him. "Kal, if I'm going to protect you, I need to know the truth. Why were you so scared that you thought death was your only option?"

No one ever asked about her past before. Regardless of her fight, fate mated her to Taber. She wanted to be honest with him, to confide her deepest fear with him. "Before my father passed, he promised my hand in marriage to someone he thought would protect me since he would no longer be able to. In the end, the man he chose betrayed me. He traded me for his own life when a shady business deal went wrong and he was head over heels in debt to a Russian company. They wanted money or they'd kill him, instead he gave them me. I think he expected them to kill me…and I wish they had."

"What happened?"

"The man I was taken to in Russia, Wesley, he was human. Through the black market he purchased one of those collars that prevent us from shifting. He drugged me, forced me to shift, and when I came to, I had the collar around my neck. It was modified so I wasn't able to shift out of my tigress form. It forced submission and wouldn't allow me to leave the grounds." Her stomach rolled and she fought the rising bile.

"Did you ever meet someone called Victor, or hear of Bratva?"

"Wesley had a brother named Victor. He was a shifter and Wesley was jealous. What does he have to do with anything?"

"We had Victor Senior's son in section four and the people who attacked today were his men. We believe Victor and Pierce contacted Kenneth, telling him you and Tabitha were sisters and were kidnapped by us and held here against your will. Kenneth was leading the men, desperate for the money Pierce paid him."

"I knew Wesley would never give up. He thought of me as a prize because he could keep me submissive." Even to her own ears, she could hear the terror in her voice. "I can't go back. I won't, I'd rather die."

Taber placed his finger under her chin, slowly guiding her to meet his gaze. "Kal, I won't let that happen. I'll protect you, I promise."

"Don't make promises you can't keep." Her fingers went back to the empty capsule hanging around her neck. "I just need another safety measure and next time, don't stop me." She shivered, more violently than the last.

Taber nestled closer and rubbed her arms. "I never make promises I can't keep. I need to inform Ty of your past. Connor, the wolf shifter, can perform his computer magic and find out everything on Wesley."

Ignoring the pain in her stomach, she pushed up, leaning on her elbow and stared at him. "I don't want everyone to know."

"The Elders have to know. Unfortunately, you play a part in everything that's happened here today. Finding Wesley might help us take down the rogues attacking your clan. You have to realize Wesley won't stop until you're dead. I'd rather it be him." He smiled. "You can't withhold valuable information like this when it can save your life and other clan members." He reached for his cell phone on the table. "I'll protect you with my life. Now rest, you're prolonging the healing."

She settled uneasily in his embrace, listening as Taber filled Ty in on the information she gave him. *Damn it!* She was a tigress and should be able to protect herself. All those years, being locked in her animal form, tortured when Wesley was in a bad mood, and locked in that awful cage when he wanted nothing to do with her. She wouldn't live like that again, no matter the cost.

She didn't realize Taber ended the call or that she was crying, until his finger brushed away a tear from her cheek. Glancing up at him, she tried to hold the tears back, but they fell faster. Finding the Alaskan Tigers clan all those years ago, she thought she had finally turned her luck around and settled in nicely. But her miserable past still haunted her dreams and destroyed the small measure of safety she thought she had.

He ran his fingers through her hair. "That's why you have the white streaks." It wasn't a question, merely a statement.

71

"Yes. I've tried to cover them with dye, but it never works. They make me recognizable, easier for him to find me, which is why I don't leave the compound *ever*. Instead, I stay hidden, and try to accept the streaks as a part of me."

"I'm glad they won't be concealed. They're unique, like you." He pressed his lips to her forehead, sending heat racing through her body. The electricity he created stole her breath.

Pressing her hand against his chest, she played with the little patch of hair in the center of his pecs. *I've always thought bears were hairy.* "Taber you know this...we can never work."

"I thought that at first too, but seeing you unconscious and near death, I know we can make it work. Kal, we're meant to be. Do you think it's coincidental I was the one who found you? Or that now, of all times, is when we find each other?" He cupped her face. "Don't deny fate without giving us a chance. We deserve that much." He pressed his lips to hers, not allowing her a chance to deny him. He tasted of honey and sunshine, making her crave more of both.

Maybe it was her near death experience, that made her through caution to the wind and return his kisses, but she did and without hesitation. She was never going to be the same after this. Life as she knew it and the woman she'd been before, would both be gone. Diving her tongue between his lips, she devoured him, getting her fill of honey. Their nakedness allowed them to forgo the necessaries of clothing removal and to indulge in their desires. The passion controlling her didn't allow her to rethink what they were about to do or to change her mind.

She slipped her hand down his chest, until she could take his already growing shaft into her hand. Wrapping her fingers around him, she slowly slid her fingers over his length.

Her body craved his touch and it had been too long since she felt the gentle caress of another. He pulled his mouth from hers and kissed a path down her neck. Sensations collided and threatened to overwhelm her when he teased her nipples. He slipped on top of her, breaking her hold on his shaft. His bulky frame hovered above her and he stared down at her, desire burning in his eyes.

He caressed every inch of her body, sending moans of ecstasy from her lips. For such a big man, he was incredibly tender, as though trying to memorize every curve of her body with his hands and mouth. Heat soared through her blood and her cat clawed under her skin, impatient and demanding. It had been too long since she had been intimate with another and her beast wanted Taber hard and fast.

He blazed a hot, wet trail of kisses across her belly and stroked her thighs with his fingertips. With every touch, she arched her hips, demanding more. She couldn't get enough of him. Nudging her legs further apart, he cupped her core. His fingers delved inside her and she met the teasing thrusts. A demanding mewling sound, she barely recognized, vibrated in her throat. Passion drove fire through her, melting the chill in her center. The trail of wicked kisses tingled over

73

her thighs. He moved his hand and replaced it with his mouth. Tiny nips and gentle licks flicked over her sweet spot, nearly driving her over the edge. She grabbed his hair, torn between pressing him closer and dragging him up. She wanted all of him.

"Taber, please I need you." Even in the sexual haze, she realized what she said and those few words changed everything. Sex would complete their mating and no going back, but in that moment she didn't care, she wanted him inside her.

"Your wish is my command, mate." He spread her legs further, giving him the access he needed before filling her slowly, inch by inch. Half way in, he slid out before thrusting back in, filling her completely with his manhood. His strokes fed her fire like tinder set to dynamite.

His hips increased pace, driving the force of each pump. The thrusts became deeper and faster, falling into a perfect rhythm, moving with such precision, as if in a well-choreographed dance. Their bodies rocked back and forth, tension stretching her tighter as she fought for the release she longed for. Upon that release, she dug her nails into his back, arching her body into his. He pumped twice more and shouted her name as they came together. Eternity stretched on until he collapsed beside her.

Her breath slowly returned to normal and Taber cradled her against him, caressing her spine with long, lazy strokes. For the first time, in a long time, Kallie's heart didn't contain fear. In Taber's arms she knew she was safe.

# Chapter Eleven

Sated, Taber cradled his mate and it wasn't long before her chills returned with a vengeance. They rocked Kallie's body with such force her health concerned him. He pulled the covers over them, drawing her closer to his body, and nuzzled her forehead. "I'm sorry," he whispered, breathing in the sweet aroma of her hair.

"For what?" Her teeth chattered.

"We should have waited until you were feeling better. I knew your body had to repair, and now you're suffering for my desire."

"A little chill won't kill me. I'm already feeling better. But more importantly, I wanted you just as much. It's been too long since I've had the caring touch of someone." She caressed his chest with her hand, playing along the contours of his chest. "Even with that said and everything that just happened between us, I still don't think we'll work. We're different."

"Species?" When she didn't answer, he added. "We aren't that different. We both want love and a family, but more importantly, we both deserve to be happy. Give us a chance, that's all I'm asking."

"How? When this is all over, your life is in Nome, and I can't leave the only security I've ever known. I'm sorry, I just can't."

He ran his fingers over her cheek, gently caressing. "My life is wherever I want to be and I want to be with you. Ty and Raja are my closest friends, besides my brothers, and I've spent a lot of time here." *Of all the times I've visited here, why didn't I notice Kallie before?* He frowned.

"What's wrong?"

"I was just thinking. I've spent a lot of time at the compound and I've never met you before. There are forty clan members. How is it possible we've never met?"

"I've...ummm..." Her voice trembled as she glanced up at him.

"Whatever it is, you can tell me."

"When I arrived here I was scared. Ty and Raja were great. They didn't force me to join the clan activities and gave me the space I needed to heal. I spent most of my time locked in this room, scared Wesley's men would find me. I don't think I saw the light of day during the first six months. I started going for a walk late at night when everyone, except the guards, were in bed. Then one day my tigress wanted to run, and I went without a second thought. I've slowly been integrating with the clan. Ty asked me to help Mark in command central and for the first time my life became normal. I still spend a majority of my time alone, but I'm doing better."

"We'll find Wesley and see that he pays for what he did to you. No one deserves to live like he mistreated you." He longed to ease the pain in her eyes. But how could he ease pain of years of abuse?

"I don't want revenge. I just want to make sure he can't get his hands on me again, and that he can never abuse anyone else." Her gaze slid to his chest. "No one should hurt like that."

"Shhh, love. I won't let him hurt you." His cell phone vibrated on the nightstand. Reaching, he grabbed it and hit the talk button in one fluid motion. "Yeah?"

"Conner found Wesley. He's dead," Ty said. "He was murdered by someone in the Bratva. My guess is if Victor Senior didn't do it himself, then he ordered someone to do it for him. No one in their right mind would go against him and kill his brother, definitely not someone in Bratva or under his control."

"That eliminates one problem." Taber smiled down at Kallie, anxious to tell her the news. She wouldn't have to retreat back into her shell.

"Connor's searching for more information, but it looks like Wesley asked Victor to help find Kallie. I don't know why it would cause his death, but we can't overlook the unusual timing. How is Kallie?"

"She's awake, but still suffering chills."

"Bethany said that was to be expected. After the chills, she's going to feel worse for a bit, like she has the flu, but that will pass within a few hours. Then she'll want to sleep. When she awakes she should return to the same shy Kallie." Ty paused. "She's come a long way in the last few months. Just move slowly with her. If pushed, she may run and hide."

He considered Ty's words, but Taber had already decided to take up residence with Kallie. She was his mate and his responsibility to protect her. "I'll tread lightly. Thank you for your concern."

"A tigress is a handful. You have no idea what's in store for you." Ty laughed and ended the call before Taber could respond.

# Chapter Twelve

Kallie sat on the only chair in her room, with a cup in tea in her hand. The last two days had been rough as she recovered from the poison, but she was finally able to get out of bed. She wished spending the last two days in bed with Taber had been more—satisfying, instead their one time lovemaking had taken any energy she had. She could only cuddle against him, unable to take advantage of the fine specimen of man she mated.

He walked from the bathroom, a towel tied low on hips. Freshly showered, his shoulder length, brown hair was still wet, and water droplets glistened off his toned chest. She yearned to run her tongue along the contours of his chest, tracing each of the well-defined muscles and worked her way lower until she could take his shaft into her mouth.

*Damn it!* What the hell was she thinking? He's a bear! Think of the children. Years ago, before her imprisonment, she knew a girl with mixed parents, and she was one of the few that could shift to both of her parents' animals. That girl received such torment from other shifters because she wasn't able to control which animal she shifted into. Kallie never wanted that for her child.

"Kallie." He drew her out of her thoughts. "Are you sure you're okay alone for a little while?"

"I'm fine. When Bethany checked on me earlier she said I'm completely healed. I'm still a bit tired, so I think I'll crawl back into bed while you're gone."

"Maybe I should stay and join you." He shot her a cocky grin.

"No." She laughed. "I need my rest and you need to get back to business." She sat her tea aside and stood. Walking to Taber, she added a little extra sway to her hips. "When you're done come home and we'll see what we can do about *this*." She slid her hand down his chest until she could feel his rising shaft.

He cupped her ass, pressing her tight against his body. "You better stop or I'll never leave and we'll end up in bed. Sleep won't be on the agenda." His voice was low and filled with desire.

Even exhausted, she wanted to wrap her legs around his hips again, and she might have taken him up on that offer if a knock at the door hadn't interrupted. "I'll answer the door while you get dress." She slapped his butt.

When she opened the door, she was surprised to find Raja standing there. "Please come in. Are you looking for Taber?" Somewhat confused as to why her Lieutenant was here, she stumbled back and allowed him to enter. *Am I in trouble for not telling them about my past?*

"Actually I'm here to see you."

Taber stepped out of the bathroom, stealing her attention away from Raja for a moment. Taber's faded blue jeans rode low on his hips, his chest still bare. She longed to feel his arms around her again. With the news of Wesley's demise, her fears were laid to rest, but still wanted the comfort of her mate's arms around her. Turning to Raja, she took the tiger by the tail. "What's wrong?"

"Nothing that I'm aware of." He smiled. "I only stopped by to let you know Mark has asked to see you. He's recovered and would like to speak with you."

The guilt of leaving Mark when things got rough shot a knife in her chest. "Ummm...okay." She had to face Mark, to apologize. "I'll stop by to visit with him."

Raja glanced over her shoulder to Taber. "Kallie, Bethany said you were concerned about your place here now that your past has come to light. I just want to eliminate those fears. We're not going to kick you to the curb. You're part of our family and we stick by family through thick and thin."

"Thank you." Relief flooded her exhausted body. When Taber gently touched her shoulder, she leaned on him.

Raja turned to leave and then stopped to face her again. "If we knew sooner we'd have done whatever we could have to stop Wesley. Now that Wesley and Victor are dead, I hope you'll begin to fully live your life. We're a family and we'll protect you. If there's anything else you think we should know, my door is always open."

"Thank you, Raja." Kallie was overwhelmed by his kindness.

He nodded, opened the door, and left.

The clan had become the closest thing Kallie had to a family, since her father passed, and she hated the thought of ever having to leave.

"I told you it would be fine." Taber kissed her cheek and wrapped his arms around her waist. "You're too weak to go see Mark now, sleep and I'll take you when I get back."

She smiled, loving the feel of his arms around her. "I'm fine."

"I know, but humor me. Kenneth is still here. I know he's in the cage until Ty and Raja can verify his information, but it makes me uneasy since he was here for you. Just stay here until I return, okay?"

"You'll owe me." She teased, rising to her tippy toes to kiss him. Their lips met and the barely banked embers of desire flamed hot again. She thrust her hands into his hair, tangling her fingers in the wet strands. When he finally lifted his head, she was breathless, and her legs wobbled. She clung to him, not wanting to let him go.

"You make it hard to leave." His breath was hot against her cheek.

"Go. I need some rest. I'll be waiting for you, so hurry back."

"Oh, I will." He kissed her again and then left.

The moment the door shut, her heart ached for him. After months of hiding away in her room, she was used to being alone, but with Taber gone just mere minutes, it was like a part of her was missing. Is this what mating is like? How do they live with the loss until their mate returns?

She fought to not follow him. Instead, she went to bed, curling under the covers, and tying to sleep, but the pillow and blankets smelled like Taber, increasing her longing. With sleep forgotten, she considered the mess she was in. She didn't want to be mated to a bear, yet she couldn't stop seeing him, from being in his arms. Her need for him was like a heroin addict needing another fix.

How could she get out of this situation? It wouldn't work, but her will wasn't strong enough to give him up. If there were a way to get out of this mating, it would free them both to find their matched mates. He could find the sow he always wanted and she could...well, she hadn't wanted anyone in her life before, but she would like a tiger of her own.

If anyone knew a way to reverse a mating, it would be Mark. She snuggled against the pillow holding Taber's scent, and called Mark.

"Hello." Mark's gruff voice filled the line.

"Mark, it's Kallie, how are you feeling? I'm really sorry about the other day."

"Kallie, it's good to hear from you. I was worried about you. Raja said you were poisoned, did one of the threats get to you?"

"Something like that. I'm still recovering, but doing better." She didn't want to explain what really happened so to let Mark believe an intruder poisoned her was for the best right now. "I need your help with something."

"Whatever it is, I'm here for you." Eagerness filled Mark's tone.

She swallowed past the lump in her throat. "Is there any way to get out of a mating?" While she waited for Mark to answer, she wondered if she really wanted to give Taber up. They were mated for a reason, even if they were different species. Could she leave the man that was meant for her? What if she never found another mate?

"Then it's true. You've mated Taber?"

"Yeah, but he's a bear."

"Girl, take the advice from an old man, don't pass on your luck. You're one of the honored to be mated. I've searched high and low for my mate, but have never found her." Mark sighed. "There's nothing you can do. Until one of you dies, he'll be your mate. Don't think distance will help because it only makes the longing stronger, and you'll go crazy with the desire for his touch. It's why mates don't travel far without their other half, and why you always see them touching. Half of your soul is missing when your mate is gone. Neither of you will be complete without the other."

The longing Mark mentioned already coursed through her body and the bear hadn't been gone long. She couldn't imagine if he went to Nome and left her behind. It's what she expected to happen when his job was done, but how would she live with the yearning she suffered with now, especially if Mark's words were true and the longing would only get worse over time. "I was hoping for better news, but thanks, Mark."

"Why? What's wrong with Taber? He's a good man."

"Nothing's wrong with him, except he's a bear. I can't risk our children not being able to control their shifting. Having one beast inside of you is hard enough sometimes, especially as a child, but having two would be impossible." She wished to enjoy being with Taber instead of fearing a connection with him.

"That's very rare. Normally the children will take after one of their parents. They aren't usually able to shift into both." He paused. "Are you're willing to give up on happiness and a mate because of a slim, maybe five percent chance, your child might shift between two animals?"

"Yes. I knew this girl, many years ago who could and it was awful for her. What kind of life is that for a child?"

"We have our own school here. There's no need to worry. The child wouldn't be ridiculed. Kallie, take my advice, don't give up on this mating. You deserve to be happy and Taber *can* make you happy. Let go of your fears. You won't regret it."

She said goodbye to Mark and placed her phone on the table. Her conversation with Mark should have eased her worries, but she was more confused than ever.

# Chapter Thirteen

Taber leaned against the wall, his hands in the pockets of his jeans while Kenneth sat before him and the Elders, explaining his story again. They'd gone through everything twice, and it still seemed like too damn little. Taber didn't care about the lack of information being produced. All he cared about was getting back to Kallie before she had time to change her mind about them being together.

He knew she had reservations because he was a bear, but he couldn't change that and there was nothing they could do about the mating. Finding her near death in the snow had wiped away his reservations, and left him with hoping to prove they could make it work. They would have to move past their differences and focus on what they have in common. Such as their support for the clan, he might not be an official member, but he was a friend of the Alaskan Tigers and in the shifter world that was as good as being accepted by them. Ty, Raja, and their mates had no issues with Taber mating Kallie, instead they seemed to encourage it. Bethany could have suggested other ways to make sure Kallie survived the healing and how to keep her warm, instead Bethany urged Taber to help Kallie.

"That's all the information I have. I don't know what else you want me to tell you." Kenneth's voice brought Taber's attention back.

"Where did you meet Pierce?" Taber asked.

"Just outside of Boston."

"You didn't find that odd, considering you live in Maine?"

"For the money he offered, I'd have met him on the moon. I told you we needed the money for my niece. A desperate man will overlook many faults." Kenneth ran his hand over his jeans. "Honestly when I took the job I didn't see the red flags. He said he got my name from one of my former clients, and needed help to find his wife and sister-in-law. Looking back, he seemed on edge, but I thought it was just a man worried about his wife. He seemed sincere in wanting them back."

"Oh, he wants them all right and it has nothing to do with love." Taber hands tightened into fists.

"Connor's working on tracing the money, to see where it came from. If Victor had a part in this, I suspect he covered his tracks. Unlike Pierce, he'd have thought of that." Ty leaned back in his chair. "Question is, what are we going to do with you now?"

"With me?" His leg bounced with a nervous twitch while his panic level seemed to reach immeasurable levels, teasing along the lines of the control they had on their beasts. Every shifter enjoyed the sensation of a little panic in their toys.

"You've served your usefulness for Pierce. He'll now want to tie up any loose ends. He can't risk you exposing him." Taber smirked.

"But, my family…my sister and niece they need me. I've been supporting them. My sister can't work because of my niece, there's no father in the picture. You can't let Pierce kill me. You have to help me." Kenneth pleaded his case.

"We don't have to." Ty stood and walked to the window. "I'd bet he has someone in those mountains waiting for you. Pierce would know it was a death trap to send anyone here. He knew where Tabitha was, because he already had people attack. But he didn't know where Kallie was because she's been hidden."

"Ty's right, we don't have to help you. We could let you leave and go on with what's left of your life. It would be better for us since you know what we are." Raja stepped to the center of the room.

"I've known about shifters for years and I've never told anyone. Why would I now?"

"Because you're desperate to save your life. You'd sell your soul to the devil to get out of this mess." Raja held up his hand when Kenneth opened his mouth. "Don't deny it. You've already proven you were desperate by working for Pierce. How did you find out about shifters?"

"During my years in Special Forces one of my men was a shifter. He kept it secret, but we were stuck together in a gun battle. He was shot and in order to live, he risked exposing himself to me. I've never told anyone about him."

Taber's stomach twisted in a knot. Something wasn't right. "If you didn't tell anyone, then how did Pierce know to hire you for this assignment?"

"It was that shifter who recommended me to Pierce." Kenneth stared at his hands on his lap. "It was a set up."

"What's his name?" Ty demanded.

"Derek Osborn. Will you please help me?"

Ty nodded to Taber, the go ahead to let Kenneth know what they had already set in motion. Taber leaned forward, making eye contact with Kenneth. "Pierce is not above using families as hostages, or worse, to get what he wants. My brother, Thorben, is already on his way to retrieve your sister and niece. They'll be taken to a safe location. In the meantime, you'll be returned to the holding cell until we've had Connor verify the new information you gave us. After that, we can help you set up a new identity for you and your family to start over."

Kenneth nodded. "Whatever I need to do, as long as they're safe."

Taber watched Raja escort Kenneth back to his cell. The man had only tried to do right by his family and ended up being wrapped up in something that could cost him his life, or worse, the life of the people he loved. They had to stop Pierce, soon.

Remembering Tabitha mentioning Robin held the key to finding Pierce, Taber turned to Ty. "Has Connor been able to trace Robin yet? Any ideas where she's hiding?"

"Not yet, but they're closing in on her. Connor said they're about two weeks behind her. They should be able to pinpoint her location within the next few days. Connor and Lukas are working around the clock. We need to get them some help before they burn out." Ty walked across the room to stand next to the conference table. "Raja mentioned things appear to be going rather well for you and Kallie. Are you planning on staying on?"

"If I did, would that be all right?"

Ty placed his hand on Taber's shoulder. "You're a friend of the clan. You're always welcome here. I was wondering because we can make a cabin available for you and Kallie. Where she lives now isn't suitable for a couple."

Taber nodded, happy Ty approved his stay. "I don't want to rush her. Right now, she'd take any excuse to push me away. The fact I'm a bear really bothers her." He shook his head. "Hell, I think if there was a way out of our mating, she'd take it in a heartbeat."

"And you?" Ty's brow rose.

"I'll be honest, at first I didn't want a tigress as a mate. But when I found Kallie lying in the snow unconscious and thought she might die, I realized I didn't care that she was a tigress. I want her and the last few days I've been trying to prove it to her." Speaking of Kallie made him desperate to return to her. He missed her touch, her smell. Damn, he missed everything about her.

"Whenever you're both ready let me know and a cabin will be provided. I'm not sure Thorben will be overly excited about your mate, but I'm proud to have you as part of the Alaskan Tigers family."

No matter what Thorben thought of Kallie, it wouldn't change Taber's relationship with her. As long as they were happy, it didn't matter what anyone thought. He'd spent too much of his life concerned with making his family happy, pleasing everyone around him. No, this time was about him and his mate, Kallie. No one else.

# Chapter Fourteen

Taber jogged through the compound eager to get back to Kallie, his body aching to touch her. His normal cravings for honey were replaced by his need for her. The bear within him was calm whenever they were together and it was the first time he experienced contentment in weeks.

Not bothering to knock, he turned the knob and pushed opened the door to Kallie's room, half-expecting to find her asleep. He was surprised to see her lying in the middle of the bed, surrounded by pillows, reading. "I thought you were resting?" He shut the door behind him.

"I tried, but I couldn't." She placed her book aside and yawned.

"Did you miss your bear, darling?"

"I guess you could say that. After sleeping next to your warm body the last forty-eight hours, I've grown used to it." When he padded toward her, tossing his clothes to the floor as he neared the bed, she grinned. "But don't get cocky, bear. I only want you for your body heat."

"I feel so used." His jeans fell to the floor, leaving him naked before her. "Maybe me and my body heat should leave you here to freeze." He teased.

"Get your ass in this bed." She whipped the blanket to the side.

He leaped on the bed, landing on his back next to her. He slipped his arm around her. "Come here, kitty."

"Kitty?" She curled into his body and pillowed her head on his arm.

"You're my kitty."

"You better watch what you say. I have claws that will tear the hide from your body. So what happened today? Were you able to find out anything from Kenneth?"

"We weren't able to gather much, just the stuff we already knew. Connor's following up on Boston to see if he can find anything. That's where Pierce met with Kenneth, and considering he lives in Maine, it has to have something to do with Pierce's location. We just aren't sure how yet." He ran his hand down her arm. "You've got too many clothes on."

"You're going to be a mate who always wants me naked, aren't you?"

"There's nothing better than your naked body next to mine. I've been thinking about running my hands over your body since I left."

He tugged her green tank top over her head. "When do you want to go see Mark? Do you want to sleep first?"

"I called Mark while you were out. He's doing fine."

He sensed hesitation in her voice. "Is there something more?"

"I asked him if there was a way to get out of a mating." She glanced down at his bare chest. "I needed to know."

"And?" He'd fight to keep her. She was his mate and didn't want anyone else.

She shook her head. "There's nothing. No matter our choice, we'll be mated until one of us dies."

"Well, mate, I have no plans to die anytime soon. I guess you're stuck with me." He gazed at her. "Ty's offered us a cabin."

"What about your family. Your life in Nome?"

"My mate is the most important thing in my life. My home is where you are. I told you before, I'm staying here to be with you. You're comfortable and so am I, there's no reason to pick up and move. The compound is safer for you than anywhere else. My family is in Nome and we can visit, but there isn't the security there that you have here. I want to be with you, Kal." He didn't care where they were, he just wanted to be with her.

"Mark also told me the girl I knew all those years ago, who could shift between both of her parents animals, was extremely rare. Is that true?"

"I've only heard of it happening once or twice, but if anyone knows for sure it would be Doc. We can speak with him to put your worries at ease. Would that help?" He tugged her closer.

"I'd like to speak with him, but it doesn't really matter. I don't think I can get rid of you." She teased. "I just don't know if I want to bring children into the situation, to have them suffer for our choices."

"Kal, let's take one day at a time. If we have children, they won't suffer. They'll be happy and there's a school here so they won't experience the torment shifters have gone through in the past. But if you decide you don't want children, we'll deal with that." He rolled to his side, facing her. "I just want you."

He claimed her mouth, running his tongue along the seam of her lips until they parted for him. Sliding his hand down her body, he twisted the waistband of her boy shorts. "These need to come off or I'm going to tear them off of you. Your choice."

\* \* \*

"Take them off." She caught her breath before biting his lower lip. She needed his touch more than her next breath. Her tigress wasn't satisfied with only one roll in the hay. She wanted the gentle caress of his touch, the warmth of his body, and the sweet taste of his lips. She couldn't get enough of him.

While their mouths devoured each other, she slipped out of her shorts, and tossed them to the floor. He had her top gathered at her neck, but in order to pull it off they had to separate, and she wasn't sure she wanted to do that.

In order to remove the obstruction, she had no choice but to move slightly from him, lifting her tank top over her head. Dipping lower, he pulled one of her already hard nipples into his mouth, teasing the tip with his tongue. She moaned as pleasure swept her body. Holding tight to her nipple with his lips, he eased between her legs and rose on top of her. His bulky frame made her feel small, protected, and shielded.

The heat burning within her didn't allow them to take time exploring each other's bodies, or to enjoy the caresses they enjoyed the first time. Their desire controlled them, forcing them to speed the foreplay, or lose control completely to their beasts. His hands slid down her body, to rest on her knees. He stared down at her, and then hitched her knees to his hips and buried his shaft to the hilt in one smooth motion. Rocking in and out, the ferocity of his thrusts stole her breath. A moment later, he found that special place within her core and ignited the liquid heat that turned her body molten. She ran her fingers through his thick hair, her scream of pleasure became a roar.

His hips increased the pace, driving the force of each pump, and she shivered with impatience. The thrusts were deeper and steady. They moved together as one, a union she never experienced before. All those years alone and abused were washed away with the love Taber filled her with. Their bodies rocked back and forth, the tension

97

tight and increasing as they sought the pleasure of release. Taber joined her explosion of lovemaking as another moan escaped her lips. He then collapsed next to her. Their legs were still entangled as she curled into his body, feeling utterly satisfied.

# Chapter Fifteen

Hours later, Taber woke to find Kallie wrapped in his arms—a vision he would never tire of. Having her pressed against him was unlike anything he ever experienced. She completed him, and with each intimate moment they shared, their mating bond would grow stronger making it impossible for them to live without each other.

He scowled at his cell phone vibrating on the edge of bedside table. He slowly lifted his arm from her waist, stretching to reach the phone. It was a text message from Ty. *New development. We need you and Kallie in the conference room, twenty minutes.*

"Dammit." Stroking her cheek with the tip of his finger, she stirred. "Kitty," he whispered in her ear.

Her sea green eyes, that he loved to gaze into, fluttered open before closing again. "Humm?"

"I know you're tired, but Ty has requested our presence in the conference room in twenty minutes."

Her eyelids shot open, fear clear in her eyes. "Why? What did I do?"

"It's okay. Ty just mentioned there was a development and they needed us." He brushed her hair away from her face. "Don't worry, whatever it is we'll handle it. I'm by your side now." He pressed his lips to hers in a gentle kiss.

When their lips parted, desire seemed to soften the sharp bite of her fear. "How can you do that?"

"Do what?" He raised an eyebrow.

"With one kiss you managed to wipe away my fear. Even if Ty would have cast me out of the clan because I didn't tell them of my past, I know I'd still be safe as long as you were by my side."

"My Kitty, I promised I'd protect you and I'll do just that and so much more. Trust me, I can be more than your protector and mate, if you let me. I'll be your lover and your friend." He kissed along the side of her face and stopped at her earlobe to breathe in her scent. She desperately needed a friend, even the loner in him recognized that.

"I think you've already proven your skills as my lover, and we don't have time for another round." She kissed him again before scooting to the edge of the bed.

He wrapped his hand around her arm, turning her to face him. "Kal, I know you still have doubts. Just give us time...that's all I ask."

100

She stroked her fingers through his hair. "Don't take this personally, please. It's hard for me to trust anyone. When you're betrayed by someone who was supposed to love you, it's hard to open your heart again."

He rose from the bed and lifted her in his arms. "I know you've been hurt, and I'll do my best to give you the time you need, but our beasts won't let us hold our desire from each other for long." He tipped her chin with his finger. "I have to know. Why would your father promise your hand in marriage when shifters mate? Rarely do any of us date before we find our mate. It's pointless, and no one wants to fall for the wrong person. It's torture to have your body belong to someone and your heart to another."

She frowned. "Dad's mate was killed shortly after she had me, by a hunter. He said he'd never mate again. Her death nearly killed him. He didn't want me to experience the same pain. He wanted me to have a normal life, and to remove the risk of losing someone the way he had."

"Why do you call her his mate and not your mother?"

"She might have given birth to me, but the woman I considered to be my mother was human. It wasn't until I started going through the change for the first time that I found out she wasn't my biological mother, or what my father and I were. By then, he'd already made the marriage arrangement and I was starting to fall in love with my groom-to-be. My father deceived me. He might have thought he was making the decision out of love, but he was selfish. I was too young and stupid to know. But it should have been my choice." She pressed her cheek to his chest.

Sadness coated her and he wished he could rinse it away. "I'm sorry, love. He should have told you what you were long before then. Shifters raised outside of a community with no support normally experience life harder, especially the children when they have to attend a public school. By not telling you about your ability he could have taken away so many opportunities from you."

"Opportunities?"

"Children, you can only have children with your mate. You can have children with a human, but only if they're your mate. With only one shifter parent the child will have a fifty-fifty chance of shifting. Whereas if both parents are shifters the child will be too."

She took a step out of his embrace. "None of that matters now." She tapped his chest. "Ty is waiting for us, so we need to get dressed."

As she padded to the dresser across the room, he had to stop from going to her. *Damn, I love the way her tight little ass sashays!* He couldn't tear his gaze away as she put on her clothes, his imagination working overtime about how he would peel them off her.

*Mating, also known as permanently horny.* He smiled before following suit and getting dressed.

\* \* \*

"You can't be serious, Ty!" Anger poured off Taber, as he stalked toward the Alpha. After everything Kallie had been through, nearly killing herself to stay out of the hands of Wesley, and now Ty was asking her to risk her life again.

"Taber, maybe we should hear Ty out. I'm sure he has a good reason for asking me to do this." Timidly, Kallie reached out to rest her hand on Taber's arm.

"Actually I do, so if you'd sit down, I'll explain." Ty held his stand, his gaze unflinching even in the face of Taber's temper.

Taber knew attacking Ty would solve nothing, but fury surged through him like lava from a volcano. "There's no good reason to put *my* mate at risk."

"Oh, but it's okay when we risk *my* mate, is it?"

Taber valued his friendship with the Alaskan Tigers, even more now that he was mated with one of their tigers, and he didn't want to go up against him. They needed to remain strong if they were going to take down Pierce and his rogues. If they began fighting among themselves, they'd never last. "Damn it, Ty, you know that's not what I meant. If you remember, I was against risking Tabitha as well. Women are protected, it's our way. If we throw that to the wind, what morals do we have?"

Kallie squeezed his arm. "Taber, please."

His gaze left Ty for a moment, shooting toward Kallie before he nodded and wrapped his arm around her shoulders. "Fine, tell us what this plan of yours is." He took a step back from Ty, but didn't sit, instead he stood there with Kallie pressed against his side, her arms stretched around his waist.

"We have reason to believe there's still a traitor to our kind, but this time we can't draw them out because the traitor is in Nome…"

"You're accusing one of my family members?" Taber cut in. Disappointment overwhelmed the anger flooding through him.

"I'm afraid so. Shadow has visions. She sees things that will come."

"Ty, I've been around long enough to know Shadow knows everything about a person if she's met them, including who their mate will be. I know her visions are true, so can we just get to the point?" Taber was tiring of the conversation.

"Very well. When we were deciding where to take Victor, and we wanted to bring him to your family cabins, Shadow had a vision there would be an attack. Someone among your sleuth would have leaked our plan. Shadow said it would be by accident, not directly, but the only way to catch them and make sure there's no information leaked, is either stop sharing any developments with your sleuth or put a plan into action to catch them. If we act quickly, there's little chance the rogues can gather enough people for a strong attack. This is why we need immediate action." Ty sighed.

"I swear if it's Thorben I'll kill him myself." Taber and his twin had been inseparable until a year ago when Thorben began keeping company with the wrong people. Thorben had always been the wild child of the family, while Taber was the responsible one. He'd hoped his twin had wised up when he was arrested for stealing a car and spent almost a week in jail before the charges were dropped due to lack of evidence. A shifter in jail was never a good thing, and they usually had to be eliminated before someone found out about their ability and exposed everyone.

"We won't know unless you're willing to go along with us." Ty dragged Taber's attention back. "If you're willing, then you and Kallie will take the helicopter to the hunting cabins in the woods with Adam. I'll stay behind with some of guards to protect the compound and the others, while a second group will follow Raja's lead and fly to the nearby landing strip. According to Shadow, once you've called your family to inform them you'll be at the cabins with your new mate, the traitor will follow. If our plan is a success everyone will be back here within a few hours."

Kallie lifted her head from his chest and gazed at him. "Taber, we need to find out where the leak is."

He detested that she was right. If his people were causing this latest issue, he needed to fix it. "Fine. I'll need to gather some weapons from Raja's cabin and we should pack a bag to make our trip realistic. I'll call my family and let them know Kallie and I are going to the vacation cabins, to cement our mating."

"I'll advise the teams, and Raja will be in charge. Unfortunately, there will be no contact between you and the teams until the attack, in case they're monitoring the radios and cell lines. Adam will be standing by when you're ready to leave. He'll need one of the other cabins in order to fly you out whenever we've caught the traitor." Ty walked to the door to leave, but turned and added. "We're trusting you to keep Kallie safe."

"I'll protect her with my life. No one will get their hands on her." When Ty shut the door, Taber wrapped Kallie in his arms. "Are you sure you're okay with this?"

"Don't worry about me. I'll be fine. Go get your stuff. I'll start packing and meet you at my room."

He wasn't entirely convinced she was okay with the plan, but instead of arguing, he nodded and held her tight.

# Chapter Sixteen

Kallie knew time was short as she hurried across the compound in search of Doc. *Damn me for wearing high heels.* Had she known she'd been sneaking around the compound behind Taber's back to see Doc, she'd have worn flats when she left her room.

*I just need security. I can't let them get me again. I can't live like that…ever.* She picked up her pace and upon arriving outside the medical suite, she paused for a moment, trying to calm her nerves before pushing open the door.

Doc, wearing his white lab coat, sat behind a microscope. "Kallie, I heard you were recovering well since Bethany healed you. What can I do for you?"

"I don't have a lot of time to explain, but I need something from you." She inhaled a deep breath, choosing her words carefully because she wasn't sure what Ty wanted the clan to know about her. "Long story short, I was held prisoner for a long time by someone. It was part of the reason they attacked the compound the other day. It's also why I drank the poison. There's no simple way to say this except I'm leaving the compound for a while and I need a security measure…just in case they capture me." He opened his mouth as if to interrupt her, but she held up her hand. "Doc please, I'd rather be dead than be tortured like a caged animal again. I can't. Please help me." Tears tumbled down her cheeks. She knew she was weak for taking the easy way out, but she *had* to have a backup plan.

"Kallie, sit down and let us discuss this." He scooted his chair from the desk and pointed to the chair next to him. When she sat, he continued. "I know about the last poison you took and I'm astonished you survived. If Galen hadn't come to us and brought Bethany into her ability, I'm not sure you would have survived. The counteragents I have for the poison would have left irreparable damage behind. To drink it again may certainly kill you."

"That's why I want it. You don't understand what it was like."

"You're right, I don't understand what you went through, but this can't be what you want. Have you talked to your mate about this? Would you give it all up when you know he'd move heaven and earth to save you if something ever happened to you?"

For the first time in a long time, words abandoned her. She had no answer.

"Are you going to answer Doc's question?" A deep husky voice spoke from behind her.

She turned to see Taber leaning against the doorframe, a duffle bag at his feet, and his arms crossed over his chest. His hair, still damp from the shower, had little curls forming, stealing her breath. "I thought…"

"When I left Raja's quarters I caught your scent heading in the opposite direction from your room. I followed it and ended here." He pushed from the doorway and walked toward her. "Now that we've found each other, you want to give it all up?"

"Taber, I told you what my life was like before. If anyone understood I thought it would be you. I can't live like that again. There's no guarantee you'd be able to find me. You might even be killed trying to rescue me. I can't take either chance." She hated being trapped between what she might have to do, and Taber.

"There's no chance involved. I'll protect you with my life. Even if something happened to me, do you honestly think Ty, Raja, and the rest of the Alaskan Tigers would allow you to remain captive? Everyone here is your family. You need to trust us." He bent to one knee in front of her, taking her hand in his. "Don't throw what we have away."

"How did you get the last batch?" Doc asked, reminding her why she was here.

"I did my research and found the best drug that would be both painless and fast acting. I ordered it online."

His eyes went wide. "You could have gotten anything online! It could have been an extremely painful way to die. Hell, you didn't even know it would kill you."

"I never thought of that, but at the time, I didn't care. I didn't have the clan. I just needed something to keep me from falling back into evil hands. It was a safety measure."

"Kallie, I'm sorry, but I can't give you anything. It's against everything I stand for. I'm a doctor. I can't be part of you killing yourself, no matter the reason." Doc rubbed his chin, his expression deeply troubled.

"He can't, but I can." Taber stood, still holding her hand. "Come." He tugged her arm, allowing her no choice but to follow. At the door, he grabbed his bag.

She followed him through the compound, the clicking of her heels against the floor punctuating their progress. She wondered where they were going and what he was thinking. She didn't have to wait long to find out. He led her around the back of the compound to the shooting range.

"Have you ever shot a gun?" He upholstered his gun and placed it in the palm of his hand.

"No. I've never even held a gun." Tears stung her eyes. "I don't think I can."

"You can, especially if it's your life or theirs. This will protect you more than any suicide pill, and it will allow you to live." He held the gun up. "Take it."

She stared at the gun, before finally shaking her head. "I can't take another person's life."

"To save yourself from being someone's pet again, I think you could. Anyone can kill when their own life is in danger." He pushed the gun into her hand. "You need to learn to shoot, and we don't have a lot of time."

"Fine." She accepted the weapon. The cold metal against her hand caused a shiver to run along her spine. She was uncertain she could kill someone even if it meant sacrificing her life. But Taber was right, it was better than the alternative, and a good skill to have. If there was an attack on the cabins, knowing how to shoot might save her life. It would give them both peace of mind. "Let's do this."

He moved behind her as she held the gun with both hands.

"Here's the safety." He clicked off the switch. He gently raised her arms. "Aim at the target down field. It's farther than we would normally start with, but we don't have time to adjust it. Just try your best." His kissed her temple. "Sorry, about the crash course. I promise when this is over and we're home, I'll help you with a proper training course. We can also work on other defenses to keep you safe. Until then you're going to have to trust me to keep you safe."

"Taber, none of this is because I don't trust you. It's a fear that eats away at me until I can't think straight."

"We'll get through it." He slipped his hand over hers. "Close your eyes, take a deep breath, and when you're ready open your eyes, focus. Look down field with your eye on the target. Keep your arms loose and steady. When you're ready push back on the trigger. The recoil on a handgun is minimal, but you'll feel a slight jerk."

111

She did as he instructed and when she fired the gun, she was surprised by how easy it handled. Shooting should have been harder, the noise louder, but it wasn't. She wasn't sure she was emotionally ready for the ability to pull a small trigger that could take someone's life nor did she ever think she would be.

"You hit the edge of the target, not bad for your first shot. This time I want you to focus on the center of his chest. That's the best place to hit a shifter if you want to hurt them, but not kill. They'll go down and give you time to get away. There are only two immediate kill shots for shifters, the head and the heart. There's no way to heal those before it kills you." He laid his hand on the small of her back, and pushed her further. "Picture Wesley down there and he's coming for you. There's no way out, and it's you or him. Then aim for the heart and take your shot."

She shook with fear from his words. She didn't want to think about Wesley, or anyone coming for her, but instead of fighting she let the memory of Wesley swim into focus. She could almost picture him, standing there waiting for her to react. He would mock her, telling her she'd never have the guts to do it, that she'd never be anything, but the animal she was. She blinked away the tears and pulled the trigger.

"Kal, you did it. Dead center in the chest." He caressed her back. "I wish we had more time to practice, but I already called my family letting them know we're going to the cabins. I'd like to be there before anyone else." He kissed her cheek, and then showed her

112

how to put the safety on again and how to reload the gun. "Do you feel comfortable enough to shoot to use it?"

"A little. I know it's better than the alternative, but to take someone's life…I don't know. What if I hit one of our people by mistake? What if I shot you?" Fear strangled her breath.

"You're not going to shoot anyone who isn't a danger to you, and I'll do my damn best to make sure you never have to pull the trigger. This is for your peace of mind. Remember, they have to get through me first." He took the gun from her and hugged her close. "We'll swing past Raja's again and see if Bethany has an extra holster you can borrow. You two are about the same size so hers should fit you. The ones I have are too large for your small frame."

"I don't…"

"While we're off the compound I want you to have it on you. You can use this gun for now and when we get back, we'll experiment with others to see if you like the weight and feel of something else." He holstered the gun and guided her back the way they came.

"It's crazy for me to go to Raja's when I should be packing." When he raised an eyebrow, she smiled to reassure him. "I won't go to Doc's office or anywhere else. We need to be going. It doesn't take two of us to get a holster, and still need to pack."

"Okay." His reluctance was clear. "I'll be there in a few minutes and we'll head to the helicopter pad." He leaned and kissed her.

She wanted so much more than just a kiss. Her beast was eager to have him inside her again, and wouldn't be happy until they were able to spend the next several days in bed together. His care and understanding was refreshing. He provided her with an alternative to captivity and death. She was surprised by her growing love for him that was far more important than the desire coursing her body.

# Chapter Seventeen

Kallie stepped off the helicopter, surveying the grounds surrounding the cabins and the beauty of the location. Alaska was one of the most exquisite places she had the pleasure of living in, but there were areas throughout the state that were more scenic than others. She decided this area was the best of all.

The campground sat higher in the mountains where there was snow no matter the time of year. The trees around the cabins glistened with a fresh layer of white powder, and the dark wood of the cabins stood out against the pristine landscape. Her heart skipped a beat knowing whatever happened here in the next few hours could change everything. She might never see this land as beautiful again, instead only as battlefield.

"Everything okay?" Taber slung his duffle bag over his shoulder, hers in his other hand.

"Yes, it's beautiful here." She glanced around, taking in the rest of the area including the other nine cabins. "Why so many cabins?"

"My family uses this area for an escape, vacation, and hunting. Sometimes there are groups of us that come together. We each prefer our own space rather than being in one house together. With seven siblings, you really need the extra space. Even now that we're older, in Nome we have our own homes, but close enough we can walk next door, and have family dinners weekly. You know, the normal family shit." He led the way toward one of the large cabins slightly higher than the rest.

"My family never did any of that stuff. It wasn't until I came to the clan I realized how people are so close. Heck, Raja and Bethany still have family dinners with Tora and her family each week. They rotate hosting weeks now that he's mated, but he still finds time for family even with his position and responsibilities within the clan. It's something I never experienced before. Dad was always too busy." Sadness wrapped around her like a thick blanket, nearly taking her down a sink hole of depression. All her life, she wanted what so many others seemed to take for granted—a loving family that cared for each other and spent time together. She had a family that never provided emotional or physical support, only to grow worse as she began her transition into her tigress.

"It's never too late. I won't tell you my family is easy to live with, but they're supportive. Thorben's a pain in the ass, but the rest of my brothers are less stressful." He sat the duffle bags on the deck, and turned to pull her into his arms. "When this mess is over, we'll go to Nome for a couple days and you can meet them. You'll be dropped

116

into the center of family drama and quality time. I can't promise you'll enjoy every minute, but there's good parts too. Mom's going to love you."

"I'm a tigress. I'm sure they want you to settle down with a sow." She realized she was slowly coming to accept that while they were different species, she didn't want it to get in the way of what they have.

"We don't always have a say in who our mates are. You and I are proof of that." He smiled. "We'll be happy, I'll make you happy." He brought her hand to his lips, gently kissing each of her knuckles. "Come on let's go inside. I want you naked."

She followed him up the three steps to the cabin's wrap around deck. He let go of her hands to grab the bags, before opening the door. When the door shut firmly behind them, she swung around to him, her tigress crying out for him. She wanted him and hated the words that were about to come out of her mouth. "Do you think now is the best time to be naked? What if there's an attack?"

"The others are already here watching the grounds, and Adam is next door. We'll be safe. I'll recognize their scent before they're close enough to be a threat."

"If you can smell them won't they smell the others?" She glanced around the cabin. The large comfortable furniture dominated the living room, with a large hearth on one wall. It would be a cozy place to spend a snowy evening. Just past the living room she could see a large updated kitchen. The cherry wood cabinets blended in nicely with the cinnamon and cream granite countertops. It was a kitchen worthy of any chef. For a vacation house, this was pure luxury.

"Our team will have their scents covered. It's a trick your clan discovered and I've never told my family. Anyone approaching will only smell Adam and us. Once they see the helicopter they'll realize why Adam's here. I have my pilot's license, but I'm not certified for a helicopter yet." He left the bags where they sat and took her hand. "Now stop worrying. I want you naked and under me. We should have a few hours before anyone arrives and I plan to take advantage of every second." He scooped her up in his strong arms and carried her to the bedroom.

The master bedroom was just off the living room and was the only bedroom downstairs. Taber explained that two spare bedrooms were upstairs. A huge bed filled most of the large room, leaving only a pathway to each side of the bed and to another room, she assumed was a master bath. The room was done in warm browns and ebony furniture. The comforter was a creamy white with brown swirls throughout. "That bed is huge. It's got to be bigger than a king?"

"Oh, it is." He smiled at her. "Bears are big and we like our space. We spend a lot of time in bed, so why not make it something we'll enjoy. My youngest brother, Theodore, he crafts custom furniture. He made the beds, dressers, and tables for all the cabins. He's the handiest of all of the siblings, not that the rest of us lack in that department, he just makes it an art form."

Taber lowered her onto the bed, before unclipping the gun holster. "Enough talk. I want you out of these clothes." He placed the holster on the night table, and then tugged her form-fitting sweater over her head. "Get out of the pants, while I get my weapon bag."

Not wanting to waste a minute, she stripped out of the rest of her clothes and let them fall to the floor. "Hurry up." She called to him. Naked she sprawled on the bed propped up on her elbows watching the door for Taber.

He ambled in, tossing the bag within easy reach of the bed, before stripping off his own clothes. "Did my mate need something?" He teased.

"I need *you* my bear. You've kept me waiting long enough."

He grinned and he slipped into the bed beside her, pressing his lips to hers. He stroked the length of her body and slid a hand between her legs in search of her core. His fingers delved inside, stealing the remaining sliver of her control. As he worked his fingers, her body moved with the motion.

She twisted her fingers through his hair, the fierce need rising within her turned into a storm. His lips tore from hers, working their way down her neck. He slipped on top of her, nudging her legs further apart with his knee.

Her cat's impatience flexed and she wrapped her legs around him, dragging him closer. "I need you," she whispered, her body full of desire and need.

119

"Unwrap your legs." He winked.

When she obeyed, he speared her with his shaft and thrust, filling her completely. Her back arched and she leaned into him. She needed him inside of her like she needed her next breath. He pulled out and she wrapped her hand around his shaft. Teasingly, she ran her fingers down his length. Feeling the hardness in her hand, she leaned into him. His erection was pressed hard between her hand and stomach. Her mouth was just above his as his hot breath caressed her face, increasing her need. "I want you."

When her hand loosened his shaft, he lowered, angling his body to the opening of her core. "You told me once, you wanted me for my heat. How do you want me now?" he asked, rubbing his hardness against her core.

"I want all of you." Impatience shivered through her, catching her breath in her throat. "Now." Her voice was breathy and full of desire.

Without further demand, his mouth found her nipple as he slid his hardness into her. She arched her body, clawing her nails into his back until she scratched him. He started slow—a pleasurable torture, an inexorable build. Her hands roamed over him, petting him, teasing him, she loved the feel of his tight body under her fingers.

"Faster." She clenched her inner muscles around his shaft, his thrusts growing deeper and faster, sending the world into a shimmering bliss. They rocked back and forth in rhythm, until she screamed for release. He pumped her twice more before pure ecstasy found them.

"My mate, I love you," Taber whispered, nuzzling against her neck, kissing the vulnerable point behind her ear.

A wave of new fear washed over her with his three little words. *He loves me.* With a deep breath she embraced that she too loved him. The determination she had to not be left in pieces if danger stole him away from her, was no reason to deny her true feelings. "I love you Taber."

# Chapter Eighteen

Dusk blanketed the room and Taber still had his arm firmly wrapped around Kallie's body. They hadn't left the bed since they arrived. He fully understood the reasons to have such large, comfortable beds and he wasn't sure if he ever wanted to move from this room. He sighed, eventually they'd get hungry and would have to go in search for food, but until then he wasn't letting her out of his reach.

The muscles in his shoulders tensed as the beast within him caught an unfamiliar sound. Someone was moving in the woods, just downwind of him so he couldn't quite pick up on the scent, but the distinct crunch of snow under their weight and the changes in wildlife let him know there was more than one body heading toward the cabin.

"Get dressed." He gently shook Kallie and slipped out of bed, pulling his jeans on.

He listened carefully as he laced his boots and grabbed his gun. Kallie dressed swiftly, her head cocked to one side. He counted at least four more bodies in addition to the first. Not bothering with a shirt, he reached into his weapon bag. "Get your gun." He strapped the knife to his thigh before walking toward her. "No matter what happens I want you to stay in here, and have your gun ready." He brushed a kiss across her lips. "I'll be back for you."

He secured the bedroom door and headed to the living room to peek outside. He had to get a superior view of the approaching threats. Squatting near the sofa, he opened the window just a crack to gain a whiff of their scent. Anything to find out what they were dealing with before danger ignited around them.

He closed his eyes, focusing only on his sense of smell. *You've got to be shitting me!* His eyes shot open, and his body coiled like a snake ready to spring into action. *Travis?* One of his brothers and someone he never suspected. *When I get my hands on that boy.*

Adam slipped through the darkness and onto the steps. "Taber, it's me."

Still in a crouched position, Taber unlocked the door and let Adam in.

"There are five of them."

"Yeah, I caught that much. Three shifters and two humans. Travis is there." His tone held disgust as he thought of his brother giving information to an enemy. He had drilled it into Travis and the rest of his brothers repeatedly—you don't betray your kind to another.

124

"Travis?" Shock marred Adam's voice. "Damn, I met him once. He seemed like a good kid. We'll do what we can to take him down alive."

"He's family, but if he tries to harm Kallie, do what needs to be done." Taber rose from the side of the window. "I need to warn her. She'll be able to smell he's my kin. If something happens and he slips past, she must know that she can't trust him." He shook his head. "I'll kill him if he goes near my mate. I can't believe he'd betray me."

# Chapter Nineteen

Kallie stood in the corner of the room, fighting the surges of Taber's pain as if it was her own. He might be in the other room, but his anger and deep sense of betrayal ate at her heart. He had entered the bedroom to tell her about his brother's betrayal, kissed her briefly on the forehead, and then returned to the living room.

How could someone betray a family member? Especially a brother. She might not have had the close family and bond that she longed for, but she would have never betrayed her family. Why was Taber's brother here? Does he still play into Wesley plan? They had to be here for her. If they wanted Tabitha, they would have attacked the compound and not here. Kallie held the gun tight in her hand, determined not to fall victim again.

She heard the footsteps of five men tramping toward them, near the cabin's step. Her heart pounded so loudly in her ears she could barely focus. *Damn it, don't fall apart now. You have to focus.* The only light in the room came from the moon shining through the slats on the window blinds. If someone entered the room, she'd have to rely only on her sense of smell, instead of vision.

She inhaled a deep breath to steady her nerves as the footsteps sounded on the porch. The gun felt heavy in her hand and she checked to make sure the safety was off. She stepped quietly to the bedroom door.

The front door crashed opened and a fresh breeze of air moved through the house. "Travis, what the hell are you doing here?" Taber called out.

Clinging to the wall, she peered through the crack in the door to see a younger and shorter version of her mate. His hair was lighter and his lack of confidence showed in his posture.

"Where is she?"

Taber raised his gun. "What do you want with her?"

"There's a large bounty on her head and I plan to collect it." Travis advanced toward Taber and she wondered for a moment if Taber would shoot his own brother.

"You'd betray your own brother, and take his mate for money?"

"I'd do a lot more than that for money. I'm getting out of here, away from you and the rest of the family. I'm tired of being smothered by everyone. I want to live my life on my terms." Travis took another step toward Taber. "Just get out of the way, brother, and no one will get hurt. You'll be free of her and can mate again."

Taber growled and glared at Travis. "You'll stay away from my mate if you value your life at all." When Travis continued to advance, Taber jumped, taking his brother down.

Kallie fought the urge to run out there, to break up the brothers, but she promised Taber she'd stay hidden until it was safe.

The floor to her right creaked, forcing her attention away from what was happening in the other room. She swung around and found a man with short red hair, glaring at her by the window. *Tiger.* Her attention, swayed to the other room, hadn't heard the window open. When he stepped toward her, she recognized him. She couldn't believe Brian stood before her. He had spent years as a pet to Wesley as well. But unlike her, he was given privileges. He could shift when he desired, but spent most of the time in his tiger form unless he had to do something for his master. Just the thought of him saying, *yes master*, infuriated her. "Brian, what are you doing here? What do you want?"

"Oh Kallie, I've always wanted you, but you were the one thing he denied me. I'm here to take you back." He leaned against the window, staring at her. "Wesley's dead and you'll finally be mine."

"I'm mated now, I'll never be yours."

"Do you think that mating will stop me?" He snarled a deep and evil laugh, pushing away from the window to stand straight. "Oh, it will hurt you to be fucked by another man, but then again your comfort never mattered. Wesley left me his house and workshop, and I've modified the collar even more. I'll be able to control your shifts

129

with a push of a button, so I can force you into your human form anytime I want to be relieved. You remember just how much control the previous collar had, well this one has so much more." Something in his hand caught the light of the moon.

She gasped. The collar! Her finger tensed around the trigger. "I won't live like that again."

"No, you won't. It will be much worse this time." He came at her with the speed no human had.

She didn't think twice, she just shot. Her hands shook causing her to miss her chosen target, but she did hit his shoulder.

"Damn, you bitch!" He grabbed his shoulder and continued to advance toward her. "You'll pay for that and when I'm done with you, you'll beg for me to end your life."

She shot again and again, tears pouring down her face. He finally collapsed to the floor and she shot one final time right between his eyes. She sank to the floor, hands shaking. The gun now empty in her hands after she used all the bullets to take down a man she once pitied.

The door flew open and Taber ran in, his gun drawn and ready for whatever he found. Scared and confused, she raised her gun, determined to protect herself.

"Kal." He stepped around the dead man, holstering his gun. "Kitty, it's me." He approached her, reaching slowly as if afraid she'd shoot him.

"It's empty." She dropped the gun to the floor. "I...I killed him."

He reached down and scooted her into his arms. "It's all right." He carried her to the kitchen, caressing her back with his hand.

"The others?" She inquired when he propped her up on the kitchen counter. He turned the tap on and ran water over the dishrag. He touched it to her cheek, but she pushed his hand away. "I don't need this."

"You might be in shock, the coolness will help. Put it against your forehead and focus on me." He pressed the cool cloth against her skin. "The others are taken care of. They're all dead."

"Not Tra..." She wanted to say Travis, but the name stuck in her throat.

"Afraid so. He shot at me and Adam had no choice but to take the shot. It was Travis or me." He ran his hand through his hair, droplets of sweat clinging to his hand. "I'll have to tell my family."

She pulled him to her, wrapping her arms around his waist and resting her head against his chest. For that moment, she forgot about the man she killed, all she could feel was Taber's pain. He lost a brother today and it didn't matter if Travis betrayed him, the loss still hurt. "I'm sorry."

"Me too." He held her to him, their bodies pressed together, and for once it wasn't about sex or their mating bond. It was just about them and the comfort they provided each other.

She clung to him and thought about the brother she never got to meet. Guilt washed over her. She was the reason behind Travis' betrayal. *Everywhere I go disaster follows.*

Movement by the door forced her to lean away from Taber. Raja and Adam placed a body, she assumed to be Travis, into a body bag. Her heart sank.

"You know none of this is your fault," Taber said when she stared at him, her questions obviously clear in her eyes. "Mates sense everything the other is feeling, no matter how out of control their feelings are. I feel your guilt, but this had nothing to do with you. He's the one that betrayed your clan, my family, and me. It was all about money for him." He frowned. "I'm sorry I wasn't there to protect you. No one caught the second scent in your room until just before the gun went off."

"That's because he was inside the window then. He was careful not to move, until he was ready to attack. I didn't catch his scent until he was already in the room." She tossed the cloth aside and clung to Taber. She didn't care that she was sitting on the cool granite countertop. She just wanted to feel his body against hers. To know he was safe, and to give him comfort as he grieved for his brother.

He tensed and shrugged out of her embrace, pulling his gun from his holster. He swept her off the counter with his free arm and tucked her behind his back, aiming his gun toward the cabin's back door.

She was tempted to ask what was going on, but kept quiet and still.

Hard souled boots cluttered up the steps and a new scent poured into the cabin. *Another bear.* Her heart skipped a beat. Another traitor within Taber's family? She wasn't sure if her bear could stand another betrayal from one of his brothers.

# Chapter Twenty

If the scents weren't different, she would have sworn it was Taber standing before them. They were identical, down to the defiance that shimmered in their eyes. He stood in the doorway, his hands up, showing he was unarmed.

"What are you doing here, Thorben?" Taber kept his aim pointed at his brother.

"I called Ty to inform him Kenneth's sister and niece were safe. He mentioned you were here. I had a feeling something was going awry. I'm only here to help. I spotted Travis with Sanchez last week and when they saw me, Travis ran off. I thought he was up to something, but I never expected..." His words trailed off as anger replaced the sadness in his tone. "Theodore called to find out when I'd be back. He needed help making a delivery and Travis split on him. I put Travis' actions together and figured he'd be here. I'm sorry I was late. I hit some bad weather flying in."

"Thorben, I want to believe you, but after what Travis did you'll understand if I find your timing suspicious."

"I might be a pain in the ass and we haven't always seen eye-to-eye." Thorben stepped in and shut the kitchen door behind him. "But when the hell have I given you reason to think I'd deceive you? To plot against you enough to get you and your mate killed? Damn it Taber, no matter our differences we're twins, I'd never do that to you."

"You haven't..."

"Damn right I haven't and I wouldn't. I've been there any time you've needed me. How could you think..."

Taber lowered his gun, but he didn't holster it. "All we knew is that there was a leak. You've kept company in the wrong crowds, how could I not suspect you might have left something slip, even if it was on accident."

"Taber, you should know I'd never risk my family, or friends of the sleuth. No matter who I keep company with, I watch what I say when it comes to shifter business."

The men silently glared at each other for what seemed like eternity. Kallie finally stepped out from behind Taber. He shot her a glare and took hold of her wrist.

"I'm not going to stay cowering behind you all night. You two are brothers, even with your differences. One of your brothers stabbed you in the back, but that doesn't mean you should start doubting all of them. Especially if we're going to Nome."

"Go to Nome? Now?"

"Taber, we need to tell your family about Travis. You can't do that over the phone. What did you think, I'd go back to the compound without you?" She pulled her wrist free and stood next to him.

"She's right." Thorben leaned against the table. "Mom deserves better than finding out about Travis over the phone."

"It's too much of risk for Kallie." Taber slipped his arm around her waist, pulling her to him. "I won't risk you."

"Your family needs you. At least go tell them, spend a little time with them and then we can leave. You have to take Travis' body home to your parents." Before he could debate further, Raja stepped in and Adam followed him.

"Thorben, it's great to see you again." Raja held out his hand.

Thorben accepted the extended hand and shook it. "You too. Sorry I wasn't here for the action."

Raja nodded. "My sympathies concerning your brother." He turned to Taber. "What are your plans? Will you be returning to the compound?"

"We were just discussing that." Kallie cut in. "If acceptable, Raja, I'd like to accompany Taber and Thorben to Nome, to return Travis' remains to their family. It's not the best time to meet his family, but as his mate I feel it's my place."

"I haven't said you could go." Taber snarled.

"Taber your family needs you, and you need your mate," Raja said. "Adam will take you by helicopter and you can return to the compound when you're ready. I'll also send Korbin with you for additional protection, but I have no doubt she'll be safe with your sleuth." Raja nodded and walked to the door. "We've dealt with the other attackers so we'll return to compound. Adam and Korbin will be ready when you are. If you need anything, call us."

Once Raja left, Taber spun around. "That was backhanded. You played the situation and your Elder to force me to take you home with me."

"You did want me to meet your family, right?"

"Shit Kal, that wasn't what I meant. I want you safe." He held her hand in his and stared at her.

"I'm safest with you, and you need me. Now let's stop arguing and get out of here before it's too late." She snuggled into him, exhausted over the day's events. Even with the sadness of the situation, and danger still looming, anxiety coated her stomach over meeting her mate's family.

"I'll take Travis' body in the airplane and meet you there." Thorben pushed away from the table, rising to his full height. "Unless you'd like to come with me and I can bring you back to get the helicopter?"

"Go ahead. We'll grab our stuff and take the helicopter. There's no need to come back here." Taber nodded at his brother before stepping around the counter with her in tow.

138

"Very well. It will take me longer to get to the plane. I'll see you there." Thorben's gaze shifted to Kallie. "I wish the circumstances were better, but it's a pleasure to meet you. My brother is stubborn and hard to live with, but he's a good man."

"Bears are always stubborn." She teased. "I have no worries he'll see my way in the end."

Thorben laughed and left.

Taber turned to her. "So that's how it is, mate? You're planning to wrap me around your little paw, are you?"

"There's always a good woman behind every man." She smiled. "If it means I have to wrap you around my paw for you to do what's right, then yes. I have faith you'll keep me safe, and I don't think your family is a threat we need to worry about. You speak of them with such love. I know if it wasn't for me you'd never give it a second thought and you'd be on that plane with Thorben now."

"You're an amazing woman." He pulled her tight against his body and kissed her forehead. "I wish you were meeting them for a better reason—at a better time." He released her and stepped back. "I'll grab the bags."

"One thing, just in case...I need more bullets." She pointed to the empty gun that lay on the bedroom floor. It wasn't that she didn't trust his family, but it was better to go armed, than need it and not have it. He nodded and padded to the bedroom to finish dressing and to gather their things. She followed and stared at the gun. Her stomach heaved. *I killed a man tonight.*

Tigress for Two: Alaskan Tigers

# Chapter Twenty-One

Tension surged through Kallie as the helicopter landed at the small airstrip on the Brown's family property. Meeting your mate's family was always a nerve-wracking experience, but add delivering the news that Travis died betraying Taber, only made the situation more tense. Stepping out of the helicopter, she zipped her thin jacket closed.

Knowing Taber was from Nome she expected him to live on the outskirts, not on an island inhabited only by the Brown family. The island was beautiful, stunning homes spaced off in the distance and plenty of undisturbed nature to make any shifter happy. Flying in, she had seen a small dock on the other side of the island, providing them easy access to Nome until the water froze.

*Damn is it cold.* She rubbed her hands together and bounced on her toes to keep warm. Because she didn't know she would be flying north, she had left her heavy winter jacket at the compound.

Taber slipped his arm around her and ran his hand up and down her arm, trying to warm her. "Nome is always colder and the breeze from the water causes it to always feel like winter here. Even in the hottest summer months the temperature barely reaches fifty degrees."

Years of being Wesley's pet had taken away her enjoyment for the cold. She seemed to have lost the ability to keep warm. During her captivity she had only been outside a few times. Taking a deep breath, she pushed those haunting memories from her mind. "I'm okay."

Before they landed, Taber had strapped addition weapons to his body and handed her a knife she had attached to her thigh. They left their bags in the helicopter with the hopes to escape back to the compound in the coming hours.

She told him they could stay as long as he needed, but he reminded her that the Elders still needed his help to find Pierce. There was also the on-going search for Robin, if the rogues got their hands on her before the Alaskan Tigers it would mean her death, and they would never find out whatever information she had, leaving them a step behind Pierce.

"That's my parents' house." Taber nodded toward the large log house sitting on the edge of the tree line. "But I thought we'd wait for Thorben. He should be there soon."

She knew he'd want Thorben with him when he told his family of Travis' death. Mates had the ability to remove physical pain from each other, but she was helpless against the grief he suffered with. She snuggled into him just to let him know she was here for him.

A plane engine hummed as it loomed over the trees, and landed on the airstrip. Moments later the small airplane shut down and Thorben stepped out, jogging toward them. He abruptly stopped in front of them, looking toward their parents' house. "I'm surprised Mom isn't out here. She had to have heard us land."

"I haven't seen anyone but Theodore," Taber said. "Four houses over, under the deck asleep. He created a cave under there for his afternoon naps. When we were growing up, Mom never allowed us in the house in our animal form. She complained we were too large and always broke something. Under the deck has always been his spot."

She followed the direction of his pointing finger and saw a sleeping bear. If he hadn't told her Theodore was there she'd have never noticed him, he blended in the surroundings so well.

"Standing around, putting this off won't make it easier. Let's get this over with." Taber kept his arm around her waist as he moseyed across his parents' front lawn. With each step his back grew more rigid, most likely apprehensive about delivering the sad news to his mother.

As they neared the house Kallie's stomach twisted in knots. This moment was very personal for a family, something she had no right to be part of. It wasn't how his family should meet her. What if they thought back of how she came into their lives and they always remember this moment? At the bottom of the porch steps she paused, forcing Taber, who had his arm still around her waist, to stop with her.

"What it is?" He frowned.

"I should wait out here. I shouldn't go in. This is a family moment. I'll wait with Adam and Korbin." She glanced over her shoulder at Adam still in the helicopter, Korbin outside leaning on it. She'd rather be freezing with them than go inside that house.

"You're family." Thorben smiled and reached for her hand. As his fingers wrapped around hers, electricity poured through her, sending goose bumps over her already chilled skin. Her hand sizzled as though she touched fire, tearing her breath away. "What the hell?" He released her hand.

Taber pushed her behind him. "She's mine!"

"What the hell is going on here?" At a complete loss for what just happened, Kallie glanced between the brothers. If she hadn't already mated with Taber she'd have sworn she was destined to be with Thorben, but that wasn't possible. Shifters only had one mate.

The brothers glared at each other.

A woman stepped out of the house, her brown hair streaked with grey, and holding a little extra around the middle of her body, but it was the woman's height that caught Kallie's attention. She stood over six feet tall. Her gaze shined at her boys. "Damn it, you two! You're not home five minutes and already fighting."

Kallie noticed how quickly the demeanor changed between the brothers. Instead of arguing with each other, they turned to their mother, both sighing and stepping next to Kallie on different sides. Electricity soared through her arms. *What the hell is going on?*

"Bring her with you. You'll need to explain what's going on between the three of you. I'll find your father and brothers, they're hunting." She sauntered down the steps and off toward the trees. Over her shoulder she hollered back. "No fighting while I'm gone."

"Explain what?" Kallie's body fought for control as a turmoil of emotions poured through her.

"Come sit." Taber held her waist and forced her forward.

She slowly climbed the steps, exhausted as if climbing a mountain. He led her to one of the wooden rockers decorating the porch. When she sank onto it, he reached for her hand. Thorben stayed back, leaning against the railing, his fingers white where he gripped the banister. He stared at her, his eyes wild and full of desire.

"Will someone please explain what the hell is going on?"

"Occasionally bear shifters will mate like we do in the wild, where there are multiple men for the same female. It is rare, but it does happen." Taber's lips pressed tight together.

Kallie's vision blurred. "No!" She knew where this conversation was going and didn't want him to continue. *As if it wasn't bad enough I found a bear as my mate, fate has decided to give me two!*

"Kal, I'm trying to explain."

"Damn it Taber, I know where this is going and I'm telling you here and now, no. This is not going to happen!" She wanted to rant and rave until she lost her voice, but deep down she knew this rare occurrence wasn't Taber's fault. Taber and Thorben had no more say

Tigress for Two: Alaskan Tigers

in this than she did, and from Taber's first reaction, he was even less happy about it than she was.

"Mating doesn't give any of us a choice." Thorben finally spoke, his tone both furious and compassionate. "From the day we're born we're destined to a particular mate. There have been cases in the past when one of the mates die the one left behind will eventually find another, but I don't care to test that theory."

"What if I refuse this?"

"Have you experienced the desire with Taber? Has the need gotten so bad that it's painful?" Thorben shoved his hands into his jeans pockets and met her gaze. "That's what it will be like if you deny one or both of us."

Taber, still holding her hand, stepped in front of her. "You're talking about sharing her. We both know that won't work. It's been years since we got along for more than a few hours and now you want to implant yourself into our lives, and take my mate as your own."

"Do we have a choice, Taber? Because I don't see one, but please enlighten me if you do."

Kallie snatched her hand, annoyance coursing her thoughts. "We don't have time for this shit. We're here to tell your parents what happened to Travis. We didn't need this now, and we sure the hell don't need you two going at it." The men stared at her, and she shook her head. "Why would I be mated to brothers?"

146

"I think I can answer that question better than my sons." Taber's mother stood at the far side of the deck.

"Mom, I'm not sure this is the best time." Taber peeled a heated glare off his brother, to look at his mother.

"Actually it's the perfect time. It will help explain this bizarre situation to your mate."

"Ma'am, I'm Kallie. I apologize for the timing."

"No ma'am here, I'm Ava." She claimed the rocker next to Kallie. "I'm afraid your current predicament is my fault."

"Mom, be serious, this has nothing to do with you. Fate makes the decision."

"Taber, you know better than to interrupt your mother. Now sit and listen to what I have to say." Ava turned her attention back to Kallie. "My mother, Annabell, was in the position you find yourself in now. My fathers were twins and both mated to her. They sought high and low for a way to break their joined matting—for something that would remove the connection, and allow them to each find their own woman."

"And?" Kallie probed when Ava paused.

"They found nothing." She smiled at Kallie. "When denying the matting the longing became excruciating. They were left with no choice than to return to my mother."

"Why didn't you ever tell us this?" Taber raised a brow.

"It didn't matter prior to now. My parents were gone before you were old enough to remember them. It seemed useless to bring up

147

something unless I had to. But know this, I loved both my fathers and was never ashamed of them." She closed her eyes for a moment. "My fathers were just like you two, but over the years they learned to work and live together. They were not only my mother's mates and her lovers, but they were also her protectors."

"So it's the twin connection?" Kallie started to understand. "But it would make more sense if the twins were close and shared willingly. These two…" She glanced at Taber and Thorben.

"These two boys can barely get along for more than ten minutes when they're together." Ava tapped Kallie's hand. "Trust me they weren't always like that. Years ago they were as close as any two bear cubs. I don't exactly know what happened, but you're just the woman to bring them together. Identical twins have the same DNA, which is why they normally end up with the same mate. It's rare for bear shifters to have twins. I was blessed with two sets, which means I believe it will be time to tell Turi and Trey what is possible for them."

"I won't share my mate." Taber stalked toward the railing.

Kallie wanted to go to him, to wrap her arms around him, and let him know that he wouldn't have to share her. But fate didn't work that way. What choice did they have? She already sensed the claws of the painful longing for Taber, and it was not something she wanted to endure again.

"Son, you don't have a choice. You might be willing to accept the pain of denying your mate, but would you put Kallie through that as well?" She turned from Taber to Thorben. "Would you, Thorben?"

When neither man said anything, Kallie broke the silence. "I've already mated with Taber."

"Child, that doesn't matter. He claimed you and that would make the mating desire clear to all of you. Thorben didn't sense it until he touched you. Now that the connection has been made it will only be a matter of time until the longing sets in." She rose from the chair. "You three need to figure things out. Take the time and then join the family for dinner. It would be nice to spend time getting to know you."

"Mom wait." Thorben stopped his mother before she went inside. "Where is Dad, and the rest?"

"Dad returned while we were talking. I heard him at the back door. I suspect he's having a shower. Your brothers will be back later. Why?"

"I'll get him." Taber walked to the door and pulled it open.

And in a few seconds the focus changed. The brothers had to break the news to their family before Kallie could even consider her own problem with the twins.

# Chapter Twenty-Two

Kallie sat at the kitchen table with Taber, Thorben, and their parents. The brothers' grief ravaged her. She could barely tell what feelings and sensations were theirs and what were hers. She tightened her grip on the mug of hot tea with honey. Ava swore the tea would help her discomfort, but she still felt like a ship lost in the turbulence of a stormy sea. Making her nerves worse, she sat between Taber and Thorben, while their parents sat across the table, waiting the news that would devastate them.

Taber began. "There's no easy way to tell you this. Travis led a group of men to the cabins tonight, to kidnap Kallie. Mom, I'm sorry, but we were left with no option. He was killed during the attack."

Kallie noticed his explanation left out the fact that Travis tried to kill Taber.

"What?" Tears fell from Ava's eyes as she stared at her sons. "Why would he do that? He didn't even know Kallie. Are you sure it was Travis?" Their father wrapped his arm around Ava's shoulders as she wept.

"I was there, and it was him. Travis had been hanging out with bad people. We haven't figured out all the details yet, but the Elders of Kallie's clan were able to trace money that was transferred from one of Pierce's accounts to Travis. He was paid good money to kidnap her." Taber retrieved his cell phone from his pocket and hit a couple of buttons before sliding it across the table. "Twenty thousand dollars was delivered into his account an hour after I called home to let everyone know I'd be at the cabin for a few days along with a couple of the Alaskan Tigers."

Taber's father, Devlin, glanced at the screen and read the information before looking back at Taber. "What would he need that money for?"

"He said he wanted to get away from Alaska, away from the family. There was nothing we could do. Travis attacked." Taber lowered his head. "We tried to detain him, but…"

Ava's sobs cut off Taber's words. "I need to see him. Where is he?" Ava begged.

"We brought him home." Thorben rose from the chair. "I can bring him in."

"No, sit down," Devlin's ordered. "We'll need to tell your brothers first. They deserve to know before they see you carrying his body." He turned to his mate, his hand gently caressing her arm.

152

"Love, why don't you lie down? I'll tell the boys. Kallie, will you see that she rests, while we talk to the rest of the family?"

Kallie rose from her chair, thankful for something to do. "Yes, sir." She walked around the table and took the larger woman's hand. "Come, Ava."

\* \* \*

In the early morning hour, Thorben sat on the porch with a beer in hand. His head rested against the back of the rocker, eyes closed. Someone passing by might think him asleep, but his thoughts wouldn't allow him rest. His mind reeled from events that happened in the last twenty-four hours.

He was supposed to be grieving for Travis and instead all he could think about was Kallie naked. The demand to mate had invaded his rational thinking. What kind of man thinks about sex when they're grieving a sibling? "No wonder Taber doesn't want me anywhere near his mate. Hell, when she has the golden child of the family, the one that can do no wrong, why would she want me? She deserves better."

He stopped mumbling when he heard the screen door swing open, but he kept his eyes shut, hoping whoever it was would think he was sleeping and leave him alone. Bare feet padded quietly on the porch and eased into the chair beside him. The fresh scent drifting through the cool breeze could only be—Kallie. *Shit*. He debated keeping his eyes shut, ignore her, and maybe she'd go back inside.

"Thorben," she whispered and laid her hand on his arm.

153

Her voice was like a caress against his shaft, making it instantly hard. He opened his eyes, meeting her gaze.

"I think we need to talk."

"What's there to say? You have Taber. You don't want another mate, right?" He pulled his arm from under her hand, not able to stand her touch any longer.

"Thorben, give me a chance. I never expected this to happen. I rejected Taber at first too. I need some time to adjust to everything that's happened."

"You think I expected this? I'd have stayed away if I did. I'd rather not be mated then have to put any of us in this situation, especially you." He set the half-empty beer bottle on the armrest of the chair.

"Your mom explained to me, even if you wouldn't have come to us now we'd have begun to suffer from the longing for each other, until Taber's touch became too painful for me because I was longing for you as well. We couldn't have changed this, and fighting it now isn't going to make the situation any easier."

He wasn't sure what to say to her, and he didn't have to because his Aunt Bev stormed up the deck heading straight for them, anger pouring off her in waves. She rushed towards them, screaming. "You bitch! You killed my baby!"

He jumped to his feet, and not thinking of the consequences of touching Kallie, he reached for her and pulled her behind him. "Aunt Bev, she's not responsible." He wanted to be reasonable and

154

respectable to the woman who was like a second mother to him and his siblings.

She rushed toward them, her claws drawn as she reached around Thorben. Determination filled her eyes, to see Kallie pay.

"You'd protect the woman who killed two of your family members?" Rage was thick in her voice.

"Stop! I won't let you harm her. You don't know what happened."

"I didn't…" Kallie's words were lost in Bev's screams.

"Don't deny it, bitch. *He* was with Travis."

Taber and his father stepped out of the house, each grabbing one of Bev's arms and dragging her away from Thorben and Kallie. Taber turned his aunt around to face him. "Aunt Bev, we don't know if John was with Travis yesterday or if he was killed."

"How dare you protect your cousin's killer?" She glared at Taber and then her brother. "I can't believe you allowed your sons to bring her here. She got your son and nephew killed, Devlin."

"Damn it, Bev, you don't know what you're talking about. Come inside and I'll tell you what happened." Devlin looked to his sons as he opened the door for Bev. "Why don't you three go to the cabin next door. Get some rest and we'll deal with everything in the morning."

Thorben stood, legs braced and arms flexed, still protecting Kallie until Bev went into the house. Only then did he relax his muscles. "Let's go next door. Dad and Aunt Bev need privacy."

155

"What is she talking about? Who's John? Was he at the cabins?" She stepped around Thorben and stared at Taber.

"Come here." Taber held out his hand and as soon as she was in reach, he slid an arm around her waist and dragged her against his body. Ignoring Thorben, he guided her down the steps.

Thorben followed.

Taber hugged Kallie close. "John is our cousin. He left with Travis shortly after I called home. They haven't seen him since. I spoke to Raja and sent him a picture of John to determine if he was there yesterday. Raja said he didn't see anyone matching John's description. They're still checking."

"If he was there, then it was his choice. Aunt Bev should have never have come after you." Thorben walked next to Kallie, longing to touch her.

"Her son might be dead. No one can imagine what she's going through, and we have no right to judge her. She's hurting and lashed out at me because she feels I'm responsible. Most people would do the same in her position."

"Kal, you have more compassion and understanding for people than anyone I've ever known." Taber kissed the top of her head. "I'm going to grab our bags. We'll spend the night and decide what to do tomorrow. Adam and Korbin are already set up in one of the other cabins."

Taber's lips on Kallie flared Thorben's irritation. *How do I stand by and watch him embrace my mate?* A moment after the question passed his thoughts, a sense of calm found him. It didn't matter that she was Taber's mate or that he had already claimed her. Kallie was now Thorben mate as well.

"If anything happens to her while I'm gone, I'll hold you personally responsible." Taber scowled at Thorben as he headed toward the helicopter.

"She'll be safe with me." Thorben nodded and turned to Kallie. "Let's go inside. It's too cold out here for you. I'll get a fire started."

He climbed the steps two at a time with Kallie lagging just behind. Thoughts of laying her down in front of the fire and claiming her filled his mind, tightened his muscles, and hardened his shaft.

# Chapter Twenty-Three

Kallie stood behind the sofa watching Thorben stroke the fire until it was raging and heating the coolness of the cabin. She wasn't sure what to say or how to make the situation easier for any of them. Taber seemed to be cold, his embrace contained a chill she hadn't known before, while Thorben acted like she had the plague whenever she reached toward him.

"Make yourself feel at home. Do you want a blanket? The house should warm soon."

"We can't go on like this. We need to talk. Sit down." When he stood by the fireplace, unmoving, she smiled. "Please, Thorben."

Sinking onto the sofa, she pulled her legs under her and waited for him to sit. He chose the chair next to the sofa. She turned to face him. "As I tried to tell you earlier, I never expected this. It's like being tossed in the middle of the ocean and not knowing how to swim. Being trapped between Taber's emotions and yours has the waves slamming into me, and I'm already barely keeping my head above water. I realize neither of you are doing this on purpose, nor is it out of spite, but it doesn't make it any less difficult for me."

"I know you have a lot to deal with, that's why I wanted to keep my distance. You need time to adjust and when you have a clear head we'll figure this out." Thorben leaned back in the chair, the firelight highlighting his strong face.

Frustration ate at Kallie. "There's nothing to figure out. Your mother has experience with this and says there's nothing we can do. In order to make *us* work, you and Taber need to work out whatever is going on because this war between you two is becoming unbearable for me."

"I don't want to make things any more difficult for you."

"It's not going to happen overnight and it's not going to be easy." She laughed. "To think only days ago I rejected mating because he was a bear...now I'm to be mated to two bears."

"You have something against bears?"

"Not exactly. I knew a girl whose parents were different species. She had a hard time controlling her shifts. She'd shift to both animals. I don't want that for my child."

"That's a very rare condition."

"So I've been told, but I'm not sure I'm willing to risk it. She was teased to a point she nearly took her life." She hugged her legs to her chest.

"Your clan has their own school which would allow our children to have the support of other shifters."

She didn't want to leave her clan's compound and Taber already said he'd stay with her. Would Thorben join them?

The door opened. Taber walked in, their bags in his hand.

"I feel your anxiety." Thorben leaned forward, taking her hand in his. "Is it the thought of having children?"

She shook her head and tapped the sofa. "Taber come join us. I need to know why you two can't get along."

Taber sat next to her, just far enough away to not touch. "Kal, I think we have more important to deal with. My brother and I can work out our issues later. You have to decide if you'll accept him and if you do, will he move to your clan. Or we can see if there's a new development that can remove a twin mating."

"I talked to Mark and he said there was nothing to stop us from mating, so what makes you think there'll be something to stop your twin?" When Taber remained silent, she continued. "I already told Thorben we'll make this work, but the tension between you is horrible. It's hard to be in the same room with both of you. I'm tired, and you don't need me to work out your issues. While I rest, you two talk." She yawned and rose from the sofa. "Thorben, I know this might be unfair to you, but Taber and I are returning to my clan. There's a cabin for us and if you wish, you're more than willing to join us. Not that I see much of a choice with the mating longing, but I wanted to give you the option. My clan is where I feel safe and with people out there trying to kill me, safety is priority."

"That's what I don't understand, why are they after you?"

"Taber will explain. I'm going to bed." She walked around the sofa and paused, not knowing where to go.

Taber understood her hesitation and pointed. "Straight down the hall, the bedroom at the end."

Following his direction, she moseyed down the hall. She hoped they could work out their problems by morning. Adam and Korbin could take her back to the compound and the brothers could stay here. She was done with their flood of emotions, and having to watch for enemies.

* * *

Thorben rose from the chair and moved to the fireplace. He glanced at pictures lining the mantel. All of the pictures were of the family, dating back to when him and Taber were closer than any bear cubs could be, with their protective mother hovering over them until she knew they could make it on their own. The problems started when she stepped back and their father guided them into manhood.

"I know our issues won't be resolved overnight. My actions over the last few years have driven a wedge between us and no words I say will undo it. I'm sorry for the shit I pulled in the past, and haven't done things that you and the family approved of, but I've always been there when the family needed me. I never meant for things to get this bad. One day I woke up and realized I screwed up. Only time and my actions will prove I've changed. Unless you give me a chance, we'll always be in this same spot." Thorben turn to his brother. "I

162

probably don't deserve a second chance and I wouldn't ask, but out war is tearing Kallie apart."

"There's no reason to tell me what *my* mate is going through. I know what she feels."

Fire splinted in the fireplace, but in Taber's eyes too. "There you go again, Taber. She's not just your mate. I don't want to fight with you. We have to figure out a way to live together."

"She hasn't accepted you yet, Thorben. I barely got her to accept me because I'm a bear."

"But she will accept me. She said that tonight. No matter how much we deny it, we don't seem to have a choice. Have you ever heard of someone being able to get away from their mate except through death?" Would his brother consider that an option?

"No, and get that confused look off your face. I'm not thinking of fighting you to the death for Kallie." Taber slammed his hand against the cushion.

"How did you know I thought you might?"

"Because if I were in your shoes I'd think the same. No matter our problems, we're brothers and we already lost one tonight. I won't lose another. Kallie would suffer too. We've seen what happens to a mate left behind. I won't risk her." Taber rose, stretching his long legs. He met his brother's gaze. "I'll do my best to keep the past in the past not only for Kallie's sake, but because I miss you. We're a good pair, and that's what Kallie needs. If we're going to keep her safe, she needs us to be the brothers we once were."

Thorben nodded. "I won't let you down."

"Good because if you do you'll be risking *our* mate."

Thorben knew nothing would change their fate. They were destined.

# Chapter Twenty-Four

Kallie woke to the sweet smell of bacon. Her stomach growled. She rolled onto her back to check if anyone had come to her bed last night, but the other pillow was untouched. She slipped out of bed, ignoring her duffle bag at the bottom of the bed, and padded barefoot to the kitchen, wearing the same clothes she had on the day before.

She expected to sense the wave of emotions from the brothers again, but instead she found them cooking, and an awareness of longing from them. "Something smells good."

"Good morning." They said in unison, as they glanced away from the stove and counter.

Realization hit her. She was mated to twins. They looked almost identical, with just small physical differences, such as Thorben's dimples were deeper than his brother's, and his hair a little darker. Taber was the more outspoken and outgoing of the two, while Thorben tended to be reserved.

She longed to go to them, to wrap her arms around them, but unwilling to stir their animosity, she denied herself the pleasure. She sat at the bar and watched them cook. *Men cooking, I could get used to this.* "It seems as though you've worked things out."

"When a woman orders her mates to do something, it's our duty to comply." Taber teased, placing a plate of eggs and bacon on the bar. "We've come to an understanding."

"That would be?" She grabbed a piece of bacon and took a bite.

"We'll deal with this mating like adults. When Mom taught us to share, we thought she meant just our toys. We never expected to share a woman, but we will. We'll rotate nights, so we each have time with you. Most important, you'll have us both to protect you." Taber smiled, dishing two more plates of breakfast.

"Are you sure?" Her question held caution.

"There are no others for us, Kallie." His hand cupped the side of her face, his palm so large it covered her cheek. "You're all we want. If you'll have us, we'll give you everything your heart desires. You'll be protected and cherished. We just want you." Taber leaned close, pressing his lips to hers.

Thorben leaned against the counter, eating. "He filled me in last night. I have some connections that might be able to help. John called, he's alive. Thaddeus, the next oldest after us, has gone to fetch him. Taber and I have decided we have to leave before they return. John's a liability, and we won't risk you."

"What about Travis' funeral?" She added a dash of pepper to her eggs.

"We don't have funerals as some do. Most of us prefer to be cremated, and instead of a service, we believe in a celebration of life. The family will understand." Taber's cell phone rang. He unclipped it from his belt and checked the caller ID. "After breakfast we'll say goodbye to Mom and the rest of the family. Thorben's already packed and Adam and Korbin are standing by when we're ready. It's Ty, I have to take this." He walked to the other room, phone to his ear.

"I know this isn't easy for you, but we're trying our best." Thorben joined her at the bar.

"I told you last night we'll make this work." She took another bite of the eggs before glancing up at him. "Taber said you've only been to the compound once, are you going to be okay staying there?"

"Neither of us cares where we are as long as we have you. I agree with Taber, you're safer there. The compound has guards and security we don't have here." He reached across the bar and laid his hand on hers. "We'll make sure you're safe, and I know your Elders are working on finding Pierce. I'll do whatever I can to see he's taken down as well. Victor Senior or anyone else won't get their hands on you. I promise." He kissed the top of her hand, just as Taber rejoined them again.

She expected to sense jealousy in Taber as she had the night before, but his calmness surprised her. They obviously reached a compromise last night.

"There's a development in Russia. Connor worked his computer genius and was able to make it sound like Victor told us his father's plans. The Russian shifters are revolting." Taber smiled and she could feel his delight. "They also believe they're only a few days behind finding Robin. Tabitha has requested Adam return to the compound soon. He'll be sent to find Robin."

"That won't be a problem. Thorben's agreed to come home with us." She grabbed the last piece of bacon from her plate and stood. "I'll take a shower and change. Then we can go see your parents." She hurried to the bathroom, anxious to feel the hot water pour over her aching muscles. The tension of the last few days buried itself deep and made her stiff. *I needed a hot shower, and one of my naked mates.* Her tigress paced impatiently inside her, demanding a shift. *Soon.* She promised.

\* \* \*

Kallie sat on the back porch with Ava, a glass of tea with honey in her hand. *These bears have never heard of coffee?* Her caffeine deprived brain and the mating heat had her edgy. She tried hard to keep her impatience down as she waited for Ava to get to the reason she pulled her away from the rest of the family. "Why did you ask to see me alone?"

168

"Having two fathers and a mother, I was always surrounded by love and understanding. I wouldn't have changed a minute of it, and I don't think my mother would have either. You'll have to make both of my boys happy. I have faith you can. My boys were raised right. They might have had some differences over the years, but they're good boys and will treat you right." She paused taking a sip of her tea. "Growing up, my siblings and I never knew who was our biological father and honestly it never mattered because they were both our Dads. I just didn't want you worrying about that when the time comes."

"I appreciate your concern." She almost told Ava she wasn't sure she wanted children, but didn't want to hurt to woman's feelings. Even if Ava wanted grandchildren it was Kallie and her men's choice. "I know I'm taking them away from you right now, but we'll return to visit soon. It's just…"

"Don't worry child. Taber already updated me on your situation. The boys want you safe, and with your clan is where you need to be." She sat her mug aside. "Come on, I know the boys are waiting for you." She took Kallie's hand and gave it a gentle squeeze. "I want you to know if you need anything I'm always here for you, and if things get out of control with whatever is going on, the family will have your back. You just call and my other boys will be there."

"Thank you, Ava." She followed Ava inside and searched for Taber. He was standing with Thorben and their father in the kitchen. She smiled at them, wanting to run to them, but held back. They seemed to have accepted the joined mating, yet uncertainty still filled her.

Adam arrived on the porch. "Adam, are we ready?" she asked.

"Whenever you and the Browns are ready, Korbin and I are." He leaned in to whisper, but in a room of shifters it was pointless. "I heard what happened with your mating. You okay?" She knew everyone heard him.

Adam was her friend. They saw each other often after she went to work in control central, but rarely discussed anything personal. "It's a little much to take in, but yeah. They're good men."

"I've known Taber for years and he's a standup guy. If Thorben's half the man as Taber then you're truly blessed by fate. Not to mention you're a special woman and deserve a good mate...or two." Adam chuckled. "That will treat you like a queen."

"Thanks Adam, I wish you an amazing mate to complement you in every way." She honestly meant it. Adam would make a woman very happy if he could only find the woman he was destined to be with.

"Are you packed and ready to go?" Taber came up next to her, placing his hand high on her back.

Thorben slipped up to her other side and placed his hand low on her back. A sense of security wrapped her like a soft, warm blanket. She savored the moment. She tried to remember the last time she was so cared for and the only time she remembered was as a child on a particularly nasty storm, curled into her father's arms. "Yeah, I'm ready."

Taber stepped away to pick up their bags, but the moment his hand left her, longing shot through her like fire. Need swept over her, buckling her knees. Thorben's arm, tight around her waist, kept her upright. She dipped closer to his body.

Her hand went to his chest with the thought of pushing away from him, but as contact was made, longing replaced distance. She wanted him like her next breath. Forgetting about everyone surrounding them, she clawed at his shirt, trying to unbutton it, but failing miserably.

"Taber, touch her!" Somewhere in the distance Kallie heard Ava's faint command.

As if being propelled by another force, Kallie pressed her lips to Thorben's, frantically diving her tongue into his warm mouth.

A hand timidly touched her shoulder and she collapsed to the floor, drawing Thorben with her. Taber bent, his hand still firmly on her shoulder.

"What just happened?" Her voice sounded strange and unlike her own.

"The mating desire. You haven't confirmed Thorben as your mate yet and until you do, you'll suffer." Ava explained. "Taber's touch will only hold the desire off for so long. I suspect with what you've displayed just now, you only have a couple hours until it's uncontrollable."

The room cleared, and relieved that she was no longer putting on some kind of show for the family, Kallie leaned against Thorben. "A few hours, can we get back to the compound in time?"

"It's risky, but if we can't control it, we'll be in trouble in the helicopter."

Taber was right. There wasn't enough room in the helicopter if the mating desire became overwhelming. What choice did they have but to stay where they were?

"Why not go back to the cabins? It will be private. I can take the plane if Adam and Korbin can't stay. As soon as this passes we'll fly to the compound." Thorben snuggled his chin into her shoulder, nuzzling her hair.

Taber seemed to consider their options before nodding. "Mom, can you ask Adam to come in?"

"Sure son. Don't break the contact. I'm not sure what will happen if you do and it might not be something you can stop again." Ava tapped her son's shoulder and then left to fetch Adam.

"Kallie, do you think you can stand? We'll try to get you to the couch." When she shook her head, Taber sat next to them, sliding his other arm around her. "We can be at the cabins within the hour."

When she glanced up at him, concern filled his eyes. She knew he was feeling her pain as the mating desire continued to bubble like boiling water just below the surface. It was suppressed, but just barely. Soon it would be upon her and there would be no way to ignore it. She longed to say something to ease Taber's concern, but fighting the desire was too much effort. Lying against Thorben, she was completely drained.

Adam stepped into the living room. "Ava said you needed me."

"We have to go back to the cabins. Kallie's mating desire with Thorben won't last long enough to get us back to the compound. I'd like you and Korbin there for protection, but if you wish to return back to the compound I can get my brothers."

"No Taber, we're at your disposal until I have to follow a lead to Robin. I'll let the Elders know so they don't expect us this evening." Adam pulled his cell phone from his pocket. "The cabins are almost an hour from here, will she make it?"

"That far yes, but we'll need to be airborne in the next fifteen minutes. We want her away from here before John gets back. My father will find out if he means Kallie any harm or if he got wrapped up in it because of his friendship with Travis." He smiled at Kallie, before turning back to Adam. "We'll bring her to the helicopter. You and Korbin meet us there in ten minutes."

A moan escaped her lips, as another wave of longing hit her. Unlike before the waves were gentler, but still took everything in her to not start grinding her body into Thorben's.

"Make that five minutes. We're running out of time." Taber squeezed Kallie's shoulder. "Come on Kallie, hold on a little bit longer."

# Chapter Twenty-Five

Kallie's head fell against Taber's chest as he carried her to the same cabin they shared before. Thorben walked beside them, close enough to keep his hand in hers. He wanted to carry her, but they all knew they might not make it to the cabin if he did. "Hurry," she cried out as another wave hit her. She squeezed Thorben's hand and her back arched. Her resolve was almost gone and when that happened, they'd be in trouble.

Minutes seemed to be hours to finally reach a bedroom. Taber laid her in the center of the bed, both men careful to remain in contact with her. They glanced toward each other before turning their sparking green eyes back to her.

"Naked! I need you...now!" She squirmed on the bed.

"I'll leave you two." Taber released her hand and pain coursed through her.

She snatched his hand back to ease the pain, but this time it didn't help. "It's not like before. We've held off for too long. I need you both."

Thorben wasted no time striping his clothes. She suspected his own yearning had stripped his control away too. Naked, he crawled onto the bed next to her and tugged her shirt up over her head. It hung from the arm where Taber still held her hand. Thorben pushed her bra to the side as his lips feverishly claimed her nipple. His other hand went to her jeans, unbuttoning them and pushing them down her legs with them went her last shred of her sanity.

"Taber, please…"

Taber removed his own clothes, only letting go of her hand when he had to. She wasn't sure, and at that moment didn't care, if Taber stripped because he wanted her or because his own yearning had become too much for him. She reached out, her hand landing firmly on his chest, needing to feel him against her. He slid on the bed, lifting her up so he was behind her, and tilted her head so he could claim her mouth. His shaft prodded her back. She wanted to turn and take it, but he trapped her against him, holding her still.

Thorben fingers slipped between her legs and teased her bundle of nerves, dragging pleasure from her over sensitized system, in hard, hot waves. She moaned around Taber's unrelenting kiss. She was captive between their bodies. Thorben's fingers thrust into her as his thumb continued to wring more pleasure from her core.

Taber's teeth grazed her lower lip and he pulled back enough to let her cries of frustrations escape.

"I need one of you inside me. Please..." They stopped and she thought they were going to ignore her demands, but Thorben quickly slipped on top of her, angling between her spread thighs, and drove into her with one powerful thrust. He gave her no time to catch her breath before he began rocking in and out.

Taber scooted from behind and knelt before her, the hard length of him jutting toward her. Without invitation, she took him into her mouth, working her way to the base. She used her hand to cup the end of the hard shaft, moving her mouth up and down the length, slowly at the tip. Taber groaned and reached to cup the back of her head. He allowed her to set the pace.

Trapped in pace of Thorben's thrusts, she fought to find the perfect tempo to allow them to work together. Their rhythm quickly synced and she moaned, knowing they were being pleasured as one, rocking together in perfect harmony, as her ecstasy began to overwhelm her. Digging her nails into the back of Taber's thighs, she held on to him as every pump sent pulses exploding through her. She came apart at the seams, her inner muscles clenching Thorben as he continued to drive his shaft into her.

Ecstasy engulfed her. Taber cried out his release. She writhed beneath Thorben, swallowing Taber juices, before another wild climax spiraled through her.

Thorben cried out as he slammed home a final time before he collapsed to the side, their legs still entangled. Taber leaned against the back of the bed, his eyes closed.

She tugged his hand, too exhausted to speak. He scooted down on the bed and her breathing slowly returned to normal. She cuddled against both bears, contented.

*Who'd have thought I'd end happily snuggling with two bears.*

# Chapter Twenty-Six

Kallie roused in a daze of satisfaction, aware of the weight of her mates huddled on her sides. She was exhausted. Since arriving at the cabin their bouts of lovemaking were only interrupted when one went in search of food. Longing to burrow back to sleep, but knowing the clan needed them at the compound, forced her up.

"What is it, mate?" Thorben rubbed his face against her hair, marking her with his scent.

"I don't want this to end, but we have to return to the compound. The Elders are waiting." *Will things change when we're surrounded by my clan?*

"There's more." Taber prodded. "You're worried about something else. I can feel your anxiety like a lead weight in my stomach."

When she remained silent, Thorben added. "I feel it as well. What is it? Whatever it is, we'll do our best to relieve your worry."

*If only it was that easy.* "I just want you to be happy at the compound."

"You don't get it, do you Kal?" Taber propped up on his elbow, staring down at her. "You're all we want. It doesn't matter where we are, as long as you're with us."

Those were the words she wanted to hear, but the nagging doubt her father drilled into her for so many years continued to creep inside her insecurities. "There was another reason I never wanted to mate. I didn't want to be tied to someone because of hormones, or because we'd produce children to keep our lines alive. I want someone to love me for me, not because of the chemical reaction our bodies create."

Thorben dragged his fingers slowly up her naked stomach, gazing at her intently. "The mating desire only brings people together, it doesn't produce love. I believe mates would eventually find each other even if our bodies didn't go through the mating desire, because we're destined to be together."

"I agree." Taber added. "Look at shifters that mate with humans, their first child has a fifty-fifty chance of being a shifter and from there the odds go down with each child. That has nothing to do with keeping the shifter genes alive. The mating desire is the same as what humans have with love at first sight, except stronger."

"Humans can get their relationships wrong, where we don't. We have to search for the one we're meant to be with, but once we find our mate, we're united until death. What could be better than spending your life with the one you're destined to be with?" Thorben used the tip of his finger to tilt her head toward him, bringing her face inches from his.

"When you put it that way, nothing." She pressed her lips against his, this time not out of desire, but because he said the right thing— what she needed to hear.

When their lips broke, Taber's hand went under her jaw and drew her toward him. "We love you for who you are, not because of desire. Never doubt that." His lips covered hers before she could say anything. "I told you before and I'll tell you every day. I love you Kallie. You're my mate and you complete me."

As if not to be outdone by his twin, Thorben kissed her shoulder. "My heart belongs to you and only you. I love you with every ounce of my being, Kallie."

She turned to him, raising her arm so she could run her fingers across the stumble that marred his face. Thorben was her quiet mate, more laid-back and willing to follow Taber's lead, and the over emotional of the two. He wore his heart on his sleeve and eagerly gave it to her for safekeeping. "I love you both more than I could have believed possible." She let her hand fall from his face. "I fought this mating from the beginning, but you two restored a part of me I didn't even know was missing. I'm whole again, and after...my past, I never thought I'd feel this way again."

\* \* \*

Traveling back to the compound drained Kallie of any further energy she had left. All she wanted to do was to crawl into bed and sleep.

She'd prefer with both men beside her, but Taber had to report to the Elders to find out where things stood.

Raja was waiting for them at the landing strip. "Welcome back. Thorben it's good to see you again."

"Thank you, Raja, same to you. Anything I can do to help please let me know. I'd like to keep my mate safe as well as do my part to keep your clan safe." Thorben shook Raja's outstretched hand.

"Appreciated. For now you can focus on Kallie." Raja slipped his hand into the pocket of his jeans and pulled out a key. He glanced at Kallie. "I need to bring Taber up to date on a few things and then he'll be along, if that's okay with you, Kallie?"

"Don't keep him too long." She teased.

"I'll do my best." Raja held out the key. "You'd probably like some privacy after all you've been though, and with two mates to protect you, we thought cabin twelve at the far end of the compound would be suitable."

She loved that section of the compound. It was close to the creek. "Thank you." She smiled and accepted the key.

"It's perfect timing for building. Our crew can get started on a new cabin. If you want to sit down with Ryan, he's the head of the construction team, and go over floor plans. They assure me a cabin of your choice can be completed within two months."

"Thank you, Raja." Happiness erupted in the pit of her stomach. *A place I can truly call home.*

"Go with Thorben and get some rest. I'll be there soon." Taber leaned down, his lips covering hers. When he pulled away she saw a twinge of jealousy in his eyes, but this time it wasn't aimed at Thorben. She knew Taber wanted to join her and Thorben at the cabin.

She rose onto her tippy toes and kissed him again. "I love you." With those three little words the discomfort eased from his eyes.

"I love you, too." He shot Thorben a quick look and nodded.

"She'll be fine. I'll see she gets some rest." Thorben waved to Taber as he walked away leaving her alone with Thorben for the first time. "Where to my mate?"

"This way." She led the way, with Korbin on their heels carrying the last few bags. She only carried her small overnight bag, while both of her men had additional bags since they wouldn't be returning to live in Nome. The thought of their belongings in those bags warmed her heart, reminding her she was stuck with them. *Not that I want to get rid of them anyway.*

Opening the door to the cabin, she was overwhelmed by the space. After living in the studio for so long she wasn't sure what she'd do with all this space. She stepped inside so the men could get out of the chilly air. She soaked in the beauty. A large cream sectional stretched in front of a fireplace, and acted as a divider to the kitchen. It was very open and airy. The creamy brown walls added character and color to the place, and drew out the warm tones of the hardwood.

She tossed her bag next to the table by the door and made her way into the kitchen. Warm honey color wood cabinets highlighted the gold of the granite countertop.

Kallie froze. She didn't cook! What would she to do with a kitchen that looks like it came out of a magazine? *Shit!* How could she feed two bears hungry when she couldn't even make toast without burning it? She had already experience their hunger for food, as well as in bed—more than once.

"Taber and I both cook." She turned to find Thorben leaning against the bar area with amusement clear on his face.

"What?" She pretended to not know what he was talking about.

"You're staring at the kitchen with fear." He teased. "Taber already told me you don't know how to cook, but don't worry, Mom made sure all her boys could cook. Heck, I can even sew, well a button. Mom wanted us to be able to help our mates with whatever they needed. She always said, the home responsibilities shouldn't just fall on the woman, she's got to rear the children."

She raised an eyebrow. "She didn't believe men should help raise the children?"

"Oh no, Mom would have killed Dad if he tried. She believed it was her responsibility to raise us, and then he would turn us into men. He took over when we were teenagers, teaching us how to build a cabin, furniture, hunt, and everything else a man should know. But when it came to discipline we were always more afraid of Mom."

184

"Your mom might reconsider me as a mate for her oldest boys if she knew what a crappy mate I'm going to be."

"Hey now." He stepped away from the bar and walked to her. Wrapping his arms around her, he pulled her to his body. "It's no one's place to judge, plus I couldn't have asked for a better mate. You have the courage to face danger head on when so many hide from it."

"Courage? I think you're talking about someone else. I have none of that."

He pulled back from her and gazed into her eyes. "You have more courage than any woman I've ever known. When you knew there was a traitor in our family, what did you do? You faced it by going to the cabins with Taber and stood your ground."

The memory came floating back. "I killed a man."

"You saved yourself."

"I killed someone that suffered as I had. He can't be blamed because he went insane from being held captive. It was hell being Wesley's pet. I can't blame Brian because he didn't know any other life."

"Brian was anything but a victim. He chose to live like that."

"No, you're wrong Thorben. It's not possible. I was there. He had a collar just like I did."

"Love, I'm not doubting you." He pulled her to him and led them to the couch. "While you were talking to Mom on the porch,

Ty called with some interesting news. Brian was Wesley's assistant. He's the one that modified the collars."

"That can't be true." She didn't want to believe the man she felt sorry for was responsible for her years of torture.

"He preferred to be a tiger most of the time and he only wore the collar to make you think he was like you, to gain your trust." He slid his hand down her arm. "Taber didn't want to bring your past back to light for you when you had everything else to deal with, but the laptop Raja brought home from the scene had all the information on it. How to modify the collars and so much more."

"I thought he was my friend. All those years we gave each other comfort, huddled together after Wesley tortured me. It was all a lie."

"I'm sorry, Kallie. Taber was going to tell you once we were settled here. He didn't want you to blame yourself for killing Brian and to think he was innocent."

"Does that mean this is all over?"

"I don't know. There's still John. We don't know where he stands and until we do, we can't rule out that he means you harm. But Brian and Wesley are dead. You don't have to worry about them anymore." He pulled his cell phone from his pocket and hit a few buttons. "Wesley came to the states searching for you. That's why Brian was here. He put the bounty on your head that Travis wanted so bad." He turned the phone toward her. "It made the front page paper. Wesley was brutally killed, hacked to pieces not even a shifter could survive." He set the phone on the cushion beside him. "Brian had pictures on his computer. His diary bragged about what he did. Victor Senior paid him to do it, but I don't think he ever thought he'd have a monster on his hands with Wesley dead. I suspect he believed as you did that Wesley had kept Brian prisoner and this was freeing him."

She laid her head in the crook of his arm, breathing in his spicy smell trying to suppress the anxiety that prickled at the back of her neck. "How did Travis get wrapped up in all of this?"

"The human I saw him with is bad news. He's into a lot of shady dealings and has been known to act as a hired gun if the money is right. He was one of the guys who attacked the cabin that night. He's also dead. It was him who guided Travis down the wrong path."

"I'm sorry. He lost his life because of me." She blinked the tears that threatened to fall.

He pressed tighter against her body. "Don't you dare blame yourself. Travis chose his path. He knew you were mated to Taber and he didn't care. Money was more important than family." A deep sadness stung his voice.

Wishing she could ease his grief, she clung to him, her eyelids falling shut.

"We should go to bed. You've had a long few days," he whispered against the top of her head.

"Just hold me." She closed her eyes as the long tentacles of sleep began to wrap around her, drawing her into their warm embrace.

# Chapter Twenty-Seven

Taber sat at Raja's kitchen table with Raja, Bethany, Ty, and Tabitha. The women's guards were in the living room, close enough if needed.

"Do you think Thorben is trustworthy?" Ty frowned.

"I do. I've unjustly doubted him in the past because he wasn't following the road I wanted him to take. He has never betrayed us and he's always been there when we've needed him. With the urgency of the situation and the loose rogues, we need the extra help." Taber squeezed honey from the bottle he was holding into his mouth. "If you doubt my instincts, know that Kallie can feel his emotions as well as my own since she's mated to us both. She'll sense any type of betrayal."

Ty looked to Raja before nodding. "Okay. But if he betrays us, it will be your hide on the line as well."

"Not to mention my mate's life," Taber muttered. "I wouldn't risk her or anyone here at the compound if I wasn't completely sure."

"Very well, bring him up to speed on everything," Raja said. "Any news from your father if we should be concerned with John?"

"Not yet. I expect to hear from him soon, and when I do I'll let you know. He's family, but if he's a threat, I want him eliminated. My mate is more important than a cousin who would betray his family. Every threat to Kallie except Victor Senior has been eliminated and it sounds as though the Russian shifters might take care of him in due time."

"He's with your sleuth. Devlin can deliver whatever punishment he finds suitable." Ty stood. "Knowing your father, I believe John will get what's coming to him if there's even the slightest belief he was involved. For now, return to your mate, bring your brother up to date on everything, and get some rest. We'll alert you if anything changes."

Taber grabbed a second bottle of honey and stood. Bethany placed her hand on his arm before he left. "We've put more in your cabin."

Tabitha laughed. "A lot more. We're taking stock in the honey trade now that we have two bears at the compound."

He smiled. She might be the Queen of the Alaskan Tigers, but Tabitha was one of the most down to earth people he had met. "Good, because we bears like our honey. Another stock market tip? The fish market, especially salmon."

\* \* \*

Back at the cabin, Taber found Thorben dozing with Kallie in his arms. "I leave you with the simple task of getting her into bed and I find you both on the couch."

"I told her about Brian." Thorben whispered to not wake her up.

"She didn't need that right now."

"I know. It just came out. I mentioned she had more courage than any woman I knew and one thing led to another. She never suspected Brian wasn't anything but another captive. I think once she gets over the shock it will help her move on. She's burying the pain of killing someone, but sooner or later it will rear its ugly head. We have to be there for her."

"I still remember my first kill." Taber leaned against the arm of the sofa. "It never gets easy, but that first kill will always stick with you. She did it to save her life and in time she'll accept that, we'll see to it. Right now she needs to rest—in bed."

"I'll carry her." Thorben adjusted to slip his arms under Kallie.

"Very well. When you're done, I need to speak with you." He watched Thorben carry their mate down the hall to the bedroom. He longed to be able to go to bed, wrap his body against her soft, warm skin, and sleep. First, he had to bring Thorben up to speed and then sleep before the mating desire hit again.

\* \* \*

Kallie woke, sandwiched between her two strong men. Both in a deep peaceful sleep while still maintaining her firmly in their grasp.

191

Were they worried she might disappear while they slept? She wiggled, trying to gain a little more room without waking them up.

Sleep still clung to her, threatening to pull her back under, but a noise disturbed her continued slumber. She was safe here—at the compound—between her men, with no concerned of the threats lurking in the shadows. She listened closer. A vibration? Taber's cell phone was vibrating on the nightstand. She rubbed Taber's arm. "Your phone."

He rolled over and snatched the phone. Barely cracking his eyelids, he read the display. "Damn, I've got to take this call. It's Dad." He slipped out of bed and walked across the room to lean on the dresser.

She missed the warmth of Taber's body against hers, but Thorben stirred and quickly filled her longing by pulling her to his body. "What's going on?"

"Your Dad called. It must be about John." Worry saturated her tone. She hoped John meant her no harm. The family couldn't take the grief of another family member right now.

"Don't worry. John's a follower, but he isn't an idiot." He kissed below her ear, working his way down her neck, biting softly where her shoulder met her neck, and then running his tongue up the length again.

Desire fluttered and she turned to face him. She ran her fingers over his chest, caressing gently through his chest hair. Her lips pressed to his. She wanted him inside her.

192

Taber cleared his throat. Thorben leaned to the side so she could see Taber too.

"Dad says John didn't know where they were going. When he learned what they were up to, he took off, wanting no part in it. I need to inform the Elders. Stay in bed, I'll be back shortly. I need more sleep."

"What's that got to do with me staying in bed?" Kallie frowned.

"I like your warm body against mine while I'm sleeping. I'll be back soon, my love."

When the door closed, Thorben pushed her back on the pillow and slipped on top of her. "I told you it would be fine." He lips claimed hers, and her desire surged.

Craving his touch, she pulled him closer. He trailed a path of hot, wet kisses to her breasts, pausing to nip and suck each one. Every stroke of his tongue fired the wild craving in her blood. When they spoke of the mating fever, she thought they were exaggerating, but the force of this primal passion consumed her. His kisses found their way back to her lips, his bulky frame hovering over as he gazed down at her, his desire clear in his eyes.

He stroked every inch of her body. Her body cried out for more. His hands stroked and teased until he found her special central core. His fingers delved inside her. As he worked his fingers, her body moved with the motion, the heat and wetness driving her crazy.

"Thorben, please I need you." She moaned, wanting to feel him inside her.

"Your wish is my command, mate." He slid between her thighs and filled her with a powerful thrust. His mouth claimed her nipple, his tongue running lazy circles around her nipple before sucking gently. Thrusting his shaft in and out of her, she clawed at his back, pulling their bodies together. She tightened her inner muscles around him, forcing him to go harder and faster. The hard, blunt force of his rocking hips drove her mad until her world splintered and she heard him roar her name. He rolled to his side, cuddling against her. Kallie's smile faded as she floated in the sea of bliss, her cat sated for the time being.

# Chapter Twenty-Eight

Days later, Kallie cuddled with Thorben in front of the large fireplace, the warm glow danced over the otherwise dark room. They were alone again while Taber attended a meeting with the Elders. Thorben had been invited, but the brothers didn't want to leave her alone, not even at the compound. The danger to her life had passed, but the clan was still at risk.

A few shifters continue to guard the grounds from the mountainside, and Mark had taken over her duties at command central until she was ready to return, or until Ty found someone to replace her. Taber and Thorben urged her to quit the position. She wasn't sure she wanted to. Her men were working with the Elders and she needed something to fill the time when they were away.

"Mate, you're a million miles away."

She smiled at him. Thorben had already proven to be the more romantic of the two brothers, cuddling by the fire, gentle caresses, sweet words of love, and the list went on. She never deprived him of the little alone time they had together. "Tell me what do you think of the floor plan I picked out?" She steered the conversation away from her real thoughts.

She had chosen a large one-floor cabin with three master suites and two additional bedrooms. This allowed everyone to have their own space, as well as two extra rooms for children if they chose to have them. Her men had convinced her that it would be better to build the extra rooms now than to wait and the season be wrong. Since their children would be interspecies no one, not even Doc, was sure how long her pregnancy would last. They'd have to wait to see which gene was more dominant. If she was to have a typical tigress pregnancy, she'd give birth in three and half months. If the pregnancy steered toward the Kodiak bears, she'd give birth seven and half months later. Either way they needed to have the additional rooms in case they were destined to have children.

The cabin would have the same open floor plan as the one they currently resided in and the kitchen that she had fallen in love with at first sight, but there were added changes to suit her men's needs. Including an additional fireplace in her bedroom, where the men would be with her.

"As long as you're happy, it's fine with me. I want our home to be the home of your dreams and as long as we're all there together, that's all that matters." He squeezed her close.

"Theodore has already agreed to make custom beds for the three master bedrooms. It will give us more room in bed." She wiggled her eyebrows.

"Oh, I can think of a few ways to break the beds in." He winked.

She laughed. "It will be a real home, and I'll have you and Taber with me."

The door suddenly swung open and Taber stepped in, a cool gust of wind following him.

"Speak of the devil himself." Thorben teased. "How did the meeting with the Elders go?"

"Very well. They believed they have pinpointed Robin's location and Adam is preparing to leave now." Taber shrugged out of his jacket and hung it on the hook. He joined them on the floor and planted a kiss on her forehead before pulling her legs onto his lap. "Robin is in a small town, Royalwood, Texas where too many shifters arriving would cause suspicion. He'll go, gain her trust, and then bring her back here. Hopefully quickly, so we can find out what she knows about Pierce."

"If it's a small town won't it raise questions if he arrives in a helicopter?" She slid her hand down Taber's arm, enjoying the touch of his skin under her fingertips.

"He'll fly to Dallas where there will be a rental car waiting for him at a private landing strip. Royalwood is a little over thirty minutes outside of Dallas. Connor speculates that the area is a whole different world."

"Poor Adam." Thorben chuckled and when she frowned with confusion, he added. "He leaves the chilly rainy weather to go to Texas, the heat capital of the states."

"I hope Robin has some information that will bring Pierce down."

"Don't worry, Kal. I don't think Pierce has any desire to kidnap you or help Victor Senior. The tiger has taken over within him and is driving him insane. He's losing control of his gang of rogues and soon he'll be alone. We've already taken out the rogues he sent after as. We're diminishing his numbers." Taber ran his hand up her jean cloaked leg.

"I'm not worried. Worrying gets you nowhere. Instead, I'm going to enjoy every moment with my two mates and live life to the fullest. We'll find Pierce."

"We're hot on his trail. It's only a matter of time." Taber tickled her calf.

"We won't rest until we do, and as long as any danger is out there, you know we'll protect you." Thorben pressed a kiss against her temple. "My mate, you're a lucky woman having two mates for the price of one."

"I couldn't agree with you more." She smiled at her men. "I never expected my life to end up so happy and satisfying. I love you both."

# Storm Queen Preview

## Stormkin Series Book One
## Chapter One

Kayla Benson leaned against the bar, fighting to keep her eyes open. Saturday nights were Stormie's busiest. Her feet ached from pulling a double after one of the bartenders called out sick.

"Boss, you okay?" Trey—the bar's bouncer—came out of the kitchen, shrugging on his leather jacket. He had stayed behind after they closed, helping her lock up.

"Sure. It's just been a long night." One that wouldn't be ending for a few more hours. The bar needed setting up for the Sunday lunch crowd, and payroll waited on her desk. *Molly couldn't have called off on a worst night. Leaving a message with one of the waitress staff, instead of telling me directly, is the last straw. She's worked her last day at Stormie's. Tomorrow I'll call and place an ad in the paper for a new bartender. Hopefully I'll have a replacement in no time.*

"You sure you don't want me to stay? I can…"

She raised her hand cutting him off. "No, thanks though. You go home. I'll see you on Monday."

"I don't like leaving you here by yourself." Trey looked dangerous, one of the main reasons she hired him, but he also had the heart of a saint. He stood six feet five, his preference of jeans and a white T-shirt showed off his corded muscles. The rough leather jacket and motorcycle added to his bad boy persona—the kind every woman wanted, the hard and dangerous appearance with a heart of gold. When he cared about someone, Trey looked out for them.

"I'm fine. I've got a few hours of payroll to do yet. Not to mention orders to place." She rubbed the small of her back doing her best to relieve the tension that had taken up residence earlier in the evening.

One hand on the side door the staff used, he eyed her. "You got my number. Call me if you need anything. I'm just around the corner and can be here in a few minutes."

"A lucky woman is going to steal you away from me one day and then where will I be?" She teased. When that sad day came, she'd be at a loss. Trey was one of the best bouncers Stormie's ever had. He managed to dispel problems before they grew out of control. "Don't worry, I'll be fine but I have your number on speed dial." She waved him off.

He nodded, and opened to door. "I checked the other doors. Everything's locked tight. Make sure this door locks behind me, and take the back steps up."

"Were you this demanding with the last owner?" Biting her tongue would have been kinder and far less careless. The former owner had been killed in the bar and she didn't need Trey's pointed look to remind her. Pushing away from the bar, she paced over to the door.

Over the last few years, her Sweetwater changed. Kayla couldn't put her finger on what caused the transformation, but there was something different about the town she grew up in. Sweetwater went from being a small town with friendly neighbors to being sinister and dangerous. After dark, people didn't venture out alone unless they absolutely had to. The sun rarely shined, and it seemed as if the gloom over Sweetwater refused to leave.

The door shut and she heard Trey try the handle once, checking that it was secured, and a couple of minutes later his motorcycle rumbled to life.

*Payroll isn't going to do itself.* She rubbed her eyes and patted the door. All secure. The hair on the back of her neck rose and she turned to find a man standing on the other side of the bar.

"How the hell did you get in here?" She spoke the words on a harsh exhale.

"That is not imperative at the moment. You must come with me."

"Like that's going to happen." Covering her anxiety with a snort, she backed up to the door. Adrenaline chased away her fatigue and she searched for the handle. "It's time for you to leave; the bar's closed."

Between one heartbeat and the next, he was in front of her. The overhead light glistened off his skin. An intangible force pushed her back against the cool metal door. Desire washed away her fear. "Who are you?" Violent, inexplicable need harshened her tone.

"That matters not."

"It matters to me. You're in my bar after hours. I have the right to know your name."

"Nightmare."

The name sent chills up her spine. "Nightmare, huh?" *Just what I need, some punk from the local gang trying to shake me down.* She looked him over. His dark grey suit cast a question on gang affiliation. *He's not the type I'd expect to be causing problems for business owners. What is he into? Maybe not a gang…could the mob have moved into Sweetwater?*

"I can bring your deepest fears alive." His rich voice sent a rush of heat through her body.

She raised an eyebrow in question. *Great, an escaped mental patient walks into the bar…can this night get any worse?*

"If you don't believe me, look down." The cool dare interweaving the words drew her gaze toward the floor—and it disappeared beneath her feet.

She stood on a steel beam hundreds of feet in the air. Frozen and unable to move, her heart thundered in her ears. Squeezing her eyes shut, she swallowed the hard lump in her throat. *This isn't real.*

She repeated the refrain, but not even the knowledge of standing in the bar dissuaded her mind from what her eyes told it. She dangled a thousand feet in the air and panic engulfed her.

"Believe me now?" He taunted.

"Please…" *I'm going to die.* A tear escaped her clenched eyes and she peeked down again, the acrid taste of bile in the back of her throat. The floor became solid once more and she collapsed. Sucking in noisy gulps of air, she tried to reconcile the insane with the real, but her mind rebelled.

"Come with me now before we're late." Nightmare ordered, his impassive visage cold and unforgiving.

"What do you want?" She choked out.

"I mean you no harm…"

"No harm? Are you out of your mind?" It took everything she had not to vomit. "You just had me dangling on a steel beam. Get out."

He squatted in front of her, remorseless. Catching her upper arm in his hand, she thought he wanted to pull her up, but froze and instead dropped to his knees beside her, his head bowed.

Alarmed further, she watched him warily. "What is it? Are you okay?"

"You're a Queen." His voice barely rose above a whisper. "A Stormkin Queen. The one I've searched for."

*See what I mean…a mental patient.* "What are you babbling about?"

203

"Come, let's get you off the floor. I'll explain." He pulled her to her feet and helped her to a nearby booth, almost reverently. "You're a Stormkin Queen."

"You're crazy." Maybe calling him on it wasn't the smartest move, but nothing that happened since Trey left seemed to resemble anything sane. She would have already fled if not for shakiness lingering in her trembling muscles. At least that's what she told herself. "You said that all ready, but I don't know what you mean. I've never heard of Stormkin and I'm nobody's queen."

"Stormkin is our race. We come from Shadow Providence; it's a parallel plane to your world. We're divided into territories as you're divided into states. Each territory has its own Queen who rules. Each territory has Enforcers chosen by the Queen to carry out her rulings. Our land is similar to how your government runs, but has harsher laws and punishments. Some rulers are unforgiving. If you disobey a Queens commands, the penalties can be severe. Shadow Mother rules over Shadow Providence as a whole, as your president rules over your land." The tidal wave of information battered her.

"But what do you mean I'm a Queen?" Kayla debated the swiftest way out a phone call to 9-1-1 or the door.

"It was prophesized long ago. A Queen, unlike any other would be born and she will take in the half-breeds, the unwanted, and the ones that are too dangerous for other monarchs to keep around. She'll return the Stormkins to our former glory and helps us defeat the Sunkins. It has been my mission to find her—you. I've searched for you my whole life. I've been sent to your realm for more than one reason but I will protect you with my life if necessary."

"I don't need to be protected," *except from you.* But she swallowed that addendum. *Don't set him off.* "I'm just a bar owner. There's no need for you to lay your life down for me, but you can get out of my bar."

"Your highness, forgive me. But we have waited for you for so long. You'll be a safe haven for those in need, a protector for those who cannot protect themselves. We need you." He stared at her from across the booth, his gaze drilling holes in her.

Her heart began to jackhammer. *Bartender slain after being trapped with a lunatic—news at eleven.*

*Stay calm. Breathe. Focus. Keep him talking.*

"How can I be a Queen to the Stormkins…I'm human? I was born *here*—I didn't come from another world—I grew up just a few blocks away." *How do I get the crazy guy out of my bar?*

"You might have been born here, but you're still one of us. Your father was one of the greatest Stormkin Enforcers. He left Shadow Providence to be with your mother—she was not a Stormkin. He gave up everything for her. You have to return to our people. Many are dying, we need you." The man—*what the hell kind of a name is Nightmare?*—seemed to genuinely believe every word he spoke.

*But who is more the fool? The fool telling the tale or the fool sitting here listening to it?*

She sat there in silence for some time, staring down at the ring her father gave her. He gave it to her on her birthday. She never thought much of that day, but her father wove a fanciful story when he slipped it on her finger. *One day a man will come for you, and you'll need this. It will provide you with the knowledge of who to trust. Trust in it, for though I won't be there with you, it won't lead you astray.*

Shaking free of the cobwebbed cloaked memory, she stared at the man across from her. *He couldn't…no there was no way Dad meant this…I finally own Stormie's…my life is getting back on track, now some guy shows up and tells me I'm from another world. This has to be some kind of cruel joke. Am I being punked?* "But how can I help, as you said I'm human?"

"Not entirely. Your mother might not have been one of us, but the blood that runs through you is Stormkin. You have abilities that you have tried to keep hidden, and yet more that you didn't know existed but being reunited with your people will bring on your abilities quicker than you ever thought possible. The ones that you have been trying to suppress need to be let free. If any of us are going to survive, we need you to be at your strongest. We have time before we must return to Shadow Providence—to the Mother Shadow—during that time we'll need to work on your abilities."

"How can there be more than one Queen?" The memory of the ring opened her mind a little more to what he was saying. Little things in her past that made it more believable. Abilities, as much as she'd like to deny them, she had at least one that came to mind. She'd hear him out, and then make the decision if she needed to call the men in the white coats.

"Our land is divided up into many divisions, each ruling their own section. They meet four times a year or as emergencies call for to discuss issues that affect them all. Mother Shadow rules over each Queen. I'm here on Mother Shadows' orders. I was not given complete instructions only that I must familiarize myself with the new Stormie's owner. I must contact Mother Shadow, to start the process of getting you a section to rule."

*Good, an excuse to get rid of him. It will give me time to talk to Dad and find out what he really meant about the ring. Or if he knows anything about Stormkins.* "Do what you must, I have payroll to attend to." Kayla scooted to edge of the booth, ready to stand.

He caught her arm before she could stand. "Do you not understand that the Stormkin people need you? You will need to find somebody to run the bar for you. You now have more important things to deal with."

"Excuse me, but who the hell do you think you are. You might be able to come in here and tell me I'm some Queen and I might just believe you." *Believe him?* She wasn't sure how she got to that part, but at least part of her believed him. He wasn't some escaped mental patient. There was a truth to his words, that even she couldn't deny, especially not when she added in the small hints her father gave her throughout her life. "But you *will not* come in here, and take away the bar that I've worked so hard for. For years, I've worked putting away every penny I could so that one day I could own this place. I'm not sure what it is that drew me to Stormie's but I won't give it up now." She rose now angry, her hands balled into fists, ready to take on the world, or at least the man before her.

"We require your help! You cannot turn your back on your people." Nightmare rose from the booth, looming over her. The weight of his gaze intimidating her. "People are suffering and dying, while they wait for the Queen that was prophesied about."

"My people? Up until twenty minutes ago, I had no idea there was another race of people. Stormkins are not my people. Where were they all my life? Were they around when I needed them? If Dad left them to be with my mother, then why didn't he return after her death? Why did we stay here?"

# About the Author

Born and raised in the Pittsburgh, Pennsylvania area, Marissa Dobson now resides about an hour from Washington, D.C. She's a lady who likes to keep busy, and is always busy doing something. With two different college degrees, she believes you're never done learning.

Being the first daughter to an avid reader, this gave her the advantage of learning to read at a young age. Since learning to read she has always had her nose in a book. It wasn't until she was a teenager that she started writing down the stories she came up with.

Marissa is blessed with a wonderful supportive husband, Thomas. He's her other half and allows her to stay home and pursue her writing. He puts up with all her quirks and listens to her brainstorm in the middle of the night.

Her writing buddies Max (a cocker spaniel) and Dawne (a beagle mix) are always around to listen to her bounce ideas off them. They might not be able to answer, but they are helpful in their own ways.

She love to hear from readers so send her an email at marissa@marissadobson.com or visit her online at http://www.marissadobson.com.

# Other Books by Marissa Dobson

Tiger Time

The Tiger's Heart

Snowy Fate

Sarah's Fate

Mason's Fate

As Fate Would Have It

Learning to Live

Learning What Love Is

Her Cowboy's Heart

Passing On

Restoring Love

Winterbloom

Unexpected Forever

Secret Valentine

The Twelve Seductive Days of Christmas

CPSIA information can be obtained at www.ICGtesting.com
Printed in the USA
LVOW05s1759170614

390428LV00024B/950/P